COURT OF DREAMS

SHADOW FAE—BOOK FOUR

C.N. CRAWFORD

CHAPTER 1

*A*ny minute now, Maddan would realize that I was standing about two feet away from him, watching as he pretended to do hot yoga.

Right now, he was sliding his hand down his leg and sticking his bum out in a half-arsed stretch. It was clear he was deriving no inner peace from this class, nor improved flexibility. Based on the angle of his gaze and the revolting bulge in his shorts, his real goal here was to stare at women's bums.

The sight before me was basically a living nightmare, and there were few things I'd rather do less than watch the Prince of Elfame sweat into terrycloth bands while sporting a semi. I may have survived years in the gladiator ring, but there was only so much horror one woman could handle in a lifetime.

Sadly, I didn't have a choice. Maddan had crucial information, and I needed to beat it out of him as soon as he stepped out of the yoga studio door.

Here was my current situation: I'd become a fugitive from the Institute, an enemy of the Shadow Fae. The knights now knew I was an angel of death. They understood that I'd hidden my true nature from them, and that I was a bit dangerous. Like, I could kill most of the earth's population if I lost my temper. It seemed these facts vexed them.

As a fugitive, I hadn't slept in weeks. I'd been moving from one flat to another, snoozing only for a few minutes at a time. See, if I dreamt, they could find me.

But even in my fevered state, I'd come up with a brilliant plan.

I needed to prove I was one of the Shadow Fae, that I belonged in the Institute, and that they shouldn't kill me. If I used Maddan to gather key information about the Institute's enemies, I could demonstrate that I was still on their side. That I was still meant to fight alongside them.

And then, I could sleep.

I blinked, fighting fatigue. Maddan hunched over in a sad approximation of downward dog.

Let the monster out to play....

I bit my lip, trying to clear my thoughts. I was at the point of delirium where I'd actually started hearing voices—particularly the mocking voice of my old gladiator master, Baleros. If I figured out how to kill him, not only could I get back in the Institute's good graces, but maybe I could silence his presence in my mind. Maddan could lead me to him, and I'd kill him. It all made perfect sense.

My heart hammered against my ribs as I weighed my options. When I attacked the prince, I wouldn't have any magic to work with. Not unless I wanted to unleash a set of black feathered wings and an outbreak of plague that would kill all of London.

I stared at the ginger prince. I had only one weapon with me: a dagger strapped to my waist, just under my jersey. Maddan, on the other hand, had proper magical weapons. For one thing, he wore a lumen stone around his neck. That meant that if he got outside, into the darkness, he'd be able to leap away from me through the shadows.

As I studied him closer, I got a better read on his magical defenses. His body shimmered with a second kind of magic —the glimmering red agony kind. If I tried to trap him in this room, around all these humans, the Prince of Elfame would take out every person in here—including a sweet-looking elderly woman in a cat T-shirt.

Our blond teacher lifted her arms over her head. "And take a deep breath in through your nose."

As she spoke, my attention was still on Maddan. I'd attack him in the stairwell away from the humans, before he opened the door to the street outside. The fluorescent lights in the stairwell would stop him from leaping away.

"And let yourself roll down, one vertebra at a time." The instructor's soothing voice filled the room. "And move down to your hands."

Maddan's gaze was fixed straight ahead, intent on a tight pair of leggings—violet, like Ruadan's magic.

At the thought of him, a hollow pain opened in my chest. I hadn't heard a word from him in weeks. He'd given me a pretty wreath, then he'd disappeared like a puff of mist in the night.

If he wanted me dead, I couldn't run from him forever. *No one* could run from the Wraith. I'd tried it once. I'd traveled miles through icy rivers. I'd woken to find Ruadan looming over me, weapons glinting. As a god of the night, sleep was his dominion. He could track me through my dreams.

We'd had our moments, sure. He'd healed me, brought me into his bed when I'd been sleeping on the floor. We'd protected each other numerous times. We'd shagged in a sewer. But the fact was, I was half death angel, and Ruadan had sworn to kill my kind.

3

The abrupt loss of him from my life felt like a jagged ravine in my chest, but I was a survivor. I could outsmart him. If I didn't dream, he couldn't find me. Ha! I was perfectly safe, as long as I allowed myself to slowly go insane. A brilliant plan, really, apart from the hallucinations, confusion, and complete inability to regulate my emotions.

My little monster.... Baleros's voice purred in the darkest hollows of my mind. *Scrambling in the dirt.*

Another piercing bite of my lip, and my attention snapped back to the yoga class.

"Exhaling out through your mouth, and let the relaxation fill your muscles." The teacher's voice re-centered me. "Arms into prayer pose, and … did you guys hear about the people who got the Plague?"

Okay. This particular yoga teacher needed to work a bit on her relaxing patter. Guilt coiled through my gut at the mention of the Plague. Where the hells had it come from? I'd let out some of my death magic when I'd tried to save Ruadan at Hampton Court Palace, but I had thought it was only a tiny bit.

"Arms over your head, and breathe out." She smiled. "Really horrific. And I've heard it's going to get worse. Like, death everywhere, all over London's streets. And moving down gently into child's pose, take a deep relaxing breath. But yeah, it's, like, people bleeding from swollen glands in their necks."

A monster like you shouldn't be on earth, should you? said Baleros's voice.

I gritted my teeth, then whispered under my breath, "Shut up, Baleros. Get out of my head."

"Okay, and now let your head hang, rolling down slowly," the teacher chirped. "And some people are saying it can make your skin rot."

I sucked in a sharp breath at this vivid description, my body now vibrating with tension.

Should have kept you in your cage under the earth.

"Get out of my head!" I failed to keep my voice down that time.

Bollocks.

Maddan's attention shot to me, and the shock of understanding shone on his pale features. He pivoted, rushing through the class toward the front of the room.

A smile curled my lips. *That's right, bitch. I'm here for you.*

I sprinted after him, weaving between the yoga students. I slammed through the door into the stairwell. Only a few moments to catch him before I lost him.

Adrenaline sparked through my veins as the prince thundered down the stairs of the old Victorian building. I pulled my dagger from its sheath, its blade pure iron.

Death magic beat in my chest like a raven's wings, and I shot down the stairs right after him. He was getting too close to the exit, nearly at the door.

Just as he reached for the handle, I snatched the back of his shirt, clenching it in a death grip.

I braced myself for a blast of his red pain magic. It took only a moment for the shimmering magic to explode from his body, and agony ripped through my bones and muscles. Still, I held onto his shirt tight, forcing myself to maintain my concentration with an iron will. Then, I slammed him against the wall, face-first. Lightning-fast, I rammed the iron dagger into his shoulder blade. The iron in the knife would stop him from summoning any more red magic. His scream echoed off the high ceiling.

Pressing him firmly against the wall, I stood on my tiptoes. "Stop screaming or I'll cut your tongue out."

"You're a sadist," he whimpered.

"I'm a monster, and you tortured me too, so I'm less

5

inclined to go easy. Now keep your voice down."

"What do you want?" he stammered.

"I want to know where Baleros is. He's an enemy of the Institute."

"So are you."

My stomach dropped. Even Maddan knew about my fugitive status? "What?" He'd caught me totally off guard.

"You're not part of the Institute anymore," he grunted. "So why do you care?"

I felt unmoored, completely lost. He was getting me side-tracked, and I pressed the blade in further. "Stop distracting me. I want to know about Baleros. I know your father is working with him. Tell me where to find him or the pain will get worse."

Maddan groaned, thrashing to get away from me.

I twisted the blade, eliciting another scream. "I said where is he, you worm!"

"I don't know!" he whined. "Baleros doesn't trust me to know his location."

I narrowed my eyes. This was actually a believable claim. Baleros was many things, but stupid wasn't one of them. "Tell me what you do know. What's he planning?"

He groaned. "Baleros is not happy that you took the mist army from him. In fact, he's furious with you."

"And?"

"Plague…" he groaned.

"What about it?" Ruadan had captured the Unholy Grail—the artifact that held my father's death magic. The Institute had been keeping it safe. So how could anyone spread the Plague when the magic could only come from my dad or me?

Maddan groaned. "Ruadan, all the Shadow Fae. They've got the Plague. They'll be dead within days."

At his words, that jagged ravine in my chest cut a little deeper.

CHAPTER 2

*M*y blood roared in my ears. "What are you talking about? How is Baleros spreading the Plague?"

"The Unholy Grail is in the Tower."

"I know that, worm." I dug my fingernails into his shoulder. "That means it's safe."

"Except that someone in the Tower knows how to unleash its magic," he said. "Baleros's agent infected the Shadow Fae. They don't know there's a traitor among them, and he's still there."

My mind screamed with panic and a sense of vindication at the same time. So this *had* been a good idea.

"The knights don't know someone in the Institute has turned on them?" I asked in disbelief.

He grunted from the pain. "They're not even looking for a traitor. All Shadow Fae think you spread the Plague. I'm surprised you're still alive. Why haven't they killed you?"

Another brief flash of vindication. I'd been *right* to be paranoid, to refuse sleep, to move from place to place.

7

Then, the reality of the situation hit me. The knights were all dying, and they definitely wanted to kill me.

"*Who* is working for Baleros? Which knight?" I hissed. "I need a name!"

"I don't know that!" he screeched. "And what difference does it make? It's too late to save them."

My knees went weak. "What do you mean too late?"

His face was mashed against the wall. "No one can reverse the Plague. No one except Adonis, and you don't know where he is, do you?"

Now Maddan was trying to get information from me. I wasn't about to give it to him.

In any case, I could find my father, maybe. If I could get Ruadan to open the portal and send me through into my old home.

"A name," I said icily.

"I swear to the gods I don't know that. I just know the Plague is already spreading, and you're too late. Baleros wants to create chaos. He wants Ruadan dead so he can get the World Key. The Plague is supposed to weaken the Wraith. Then, Baleros's agent will kill him as soon as he gets the chance. He'll cut the key off his corpse."

A wild surge of protectiveness rippled through me. Maybe the Shadow Fae wanted me dead, but I had to warn Ruadan about the truth. I just needed more details.

I pushed Maddan hard against the wall. "Tell me anything you know about the traitor. Anything at all."

"I don't know. I don't—"

A scream from the stairs cut through the interrogation. I glanced at the elderly woman in the cat T-shirt.

"Murderer!" she shrieked. In her panic, she dropped the yoga mat from under her arm.

Bloody hells. I couldn't imagine why I'd liked her earlier.

"Stay where you are!" I shouted at her.

I couldn't deal with both of these screaming people at once. I had to keep Maddan pinned or he'd slip away into the shadows outside.

Cat Lady was still screaming, her shrieks deafening me.

Let the monster out....

My breath sped up as I started losing control. "What's his entire plan, Maddan?" I shouted.

"I told you. Spread the Plague. Get the World Key. Take over the Institute."

"Why is he so hells-bent on doing this?"

"Because!" Maddan shouted impatiently. "If he can open and control the worlds, he can use his power to control the demons trapped within them. He can conscript them to join his army, offering them freedom in return for their swords. He wants to rule the world. It's not complicated."

Dread slid through my bones. "What else do you know?"

"He won't fail. Now, he has a powerful ally on his side."

"The person in the Institute? Who?" I barked.

"Someone you know very well—"

The creaking of the door made my heart skip a beat. Cat Lady had slipped past us and opened it. Maddan craned his head to look outside, into the shadows.

It was enough. I felt the electrical rush of shadow magic from his lumen stone, the whoosh of air as he leapt past me. The knife in his shoulder blade had torn his flesh when he'd jumped. I held nothing but the gore-soaked weapon now.

I stepped outside, onto the main road. Cat Lady was running down the pavement, screaming into her mobile phone. Maddan was nowhere to be found. Six of my mist soldiers milled around the sidewalk, but they hadn't been able to stop Maddan's leap.

I loosed a sigh, rubbing a knot in my forehead. My muscles burned and dizziness clouded my thoughts.

The Shadow Fae were all dying of the Plague—and they thought it was my fault.

My days were numbered—but so were those of all the Shadow Fae. If I could get to Ruadan and speak to him, maybe I could convince him of the truth. We could find my dad together. It was the only way to move forward.

* * *

CIARA SAT NEXT to a human on a white leather sofa. His name was Jared.

I paced in front of them, wringing my hands as I did. My body buzzed with nervous energy. I'd sent a message to the Institute, explaining clearly that I had crucial information they needed to hear. Now, I only had to wait to hear back from them.

Jared let out a sigh, staring at me dreamily. "Amazing to have real supernaturals here." A blond wig was draped over his wool sweater, and a set of plastic ears poked through the hair. The whole enormous room smelled of stale cigarettes, incense, and sweat. "Legally, I'm not allowed to be in a room with women unsupervised, but I don't think the rules apply to your kind."

I pivoted, turning the other way. "Good to know."

Jared was one of those humans who had a total hard-on for the fae. He believed he was meant to be one of us, but the gods had messed it up. He was thrilled to let Ciara and me stay in his luxurious but stinking apartment for a night. Embarrassingly, he actually knew more of the Ancient Fae language than I did, and he'd started teaching me the few commands I needed to really control the mist army.

Apart from the stench, Jared's flat was a perfect hideout. It offered a balcony view of the Institute's gatehouse—just on the other side of the stone courtyard. We were so close that the golden glow of the moat beamed onto his hardwood floors through his balcony windows.

I turned to the balcony windows again, staring out. The Institute's battlements seemed to rise from a cloud of fog, and the moat's golden light streamed through the mist in perfect rays.

My throat tightened as I thought of what was going on behind those Tower walls: Shadow Fae dying in the Institute, cursing me with their final breaths.

A sharp crack of pain pierced my chest. I'd only unleashed my death angel side to save Ruadan—I never would have tried to hurt him. I wouldn't harm the other Shadow Fae, either.

It stung that Ruadan believed I'd poison them on purpose. Is that what he thought of me? That I was some sort of a—

A monster like you....

"Shut up, Baleros," I muttered.

The betrayal was eating at me like a cancer. In the depths of my mind, Ruadan's perfect features began to merge with Baleros's rugged face.

"I need to talk to Ruadan right away." I slid the balcony door open, and the chilly wind rushed over my skin. Mist floated in on the breeze and coiled around me.

"Liora."

I turned to find Jared lifting his wine.

"Ye mighty faestress! Please partake in mead with me as we dine together, we fae." He looked at me hopefully, eyebrows raised.

I scowled, grabbing a bottle of whiskey off his marble countertop. "First of all, you don't have mead. Second of all, faestress is not a word. Next of all, mead is gross, and I would never drink it. What number were we on? It doesn't matter. The point is, please stop talking, because I'm busy thinking about death and betrayal."

He raised his arms. "O wild spiritess of the oaks—"

My lip curled, and I growled at him, letting my canines show.

He fell completely silent, paling. Mist skimmed over his floor and his sofa.

Ciara frowned at me. "Stop scaring the rich human. And stop worrying. Once the note gets to Ruadan, he'll get right back to you. He knows you wouldn't hurt him. You'll be back in the Institute in no time. What can you see out there?"

"Whole lot of fog." That was the problem with the mist soldiers. You could never see shit.

I could beckon them to me at any moment by whispering a particular spell, but I tried to stay patient. They had to get the message to Ruadan. I'd included just enough details that he'd understand the urgency of the situation, but not so many that they could fall into the wrong hands.

I turned back to the balcony, hovering in the doorway. How sick was Ruadan? I could only hope his demigod nature gave him added protection. After all, that's how he'd survived my blast of death magic, years ago.

But any amount of weakness could provide an assassination opportunity to the traitor.

The great, ancient fae warrior was vulnerable in the Institute, and I had to keep him safe.

CHAPTER 3

"*F*orsooth, thine friend speaks the truth." Jared leaned back on his sofa, spreading out his arms. "Thou will be back within ye old stone walls within no time."

Had there been a time when I'd been nice to humans? Back when I'd donated a bottle of hand lotion every week to the woman in my squat, or when I'd tolerated Uncle Darrell's stories about sticking his dick in the forest soil. Those days felt like centuries ago. Now, I felt the monster inside rattling the bars of its cage, straining at the leash. Human deaths would feed my strength.

Once, I could spend a Friday night drinking cheap beer with humans, listening to Taylor Swift. Now, death fluttered between my ribs like dark moths, and I yearned to taste the blood of mortals.

Never meant to walk the earth....

"Faestress, can I touch your skin?" asked Jared.

"Quiet, mortal," I snarled. He'd be so easy to kill....

When in my life had I ever uttered the phrase *quiet, mortal?* Sometime after I'd let my angel wings out, phrases like that had just started rolling off the tongue.

Darkness spilled into my mind like ink. I pivoted, pacing again.

How had my father managed to control this power for thousands of years? Oh—that was right. He hadn't controlled the power. That's how Ruadan's wife had died. And also half of Europe.

A monster like you....

I stepped out onto the balcony, goosebumps rising on my skin in the damp air. The briny scent of the river floated over me, and I strained to see through all the fog. Were my soldiers at the gate now?

I took a long sip of whiskey, hoping for a brief bubble of inner peace. Could the whiskey drown out Baleros's voice in my head?

Should never have been born. An abomination.

Jared was still prattling on behind me. "We will celebrate the Old Gods by drinking of their bounteous gifts!"

I'll turn your body to ash, Jared. How about that?

Although I couldn't see the base of the gatehouse, I was sure that the mist soldiers would have delivered the message by now. They should be moving through the ancient doors and over the moat of light, into the Institute itself. With any luck, Ruadan would see that I told the truth. He'd know that I'd never tried to hurt him.

At least, not since the time I stabbed him.

"They've got to get back here soon, right?" asked Ciara.

"I don't know. Ruadan has sort of ghosted me recently."

Loneliness corroded me. I'd never told him how I really felt. Was it too late now? The weight of unspoken words pressed on me like a ton of craggy rocks. The assassin might have already killed him, and I'd never told him the truth.

I hugged myself, staring at the fortress. It's not like I could just barge in there. I wouldn't be able to get beyond that bloody golden moat without an invitation.

Fatigue seeped into my brain like a toxin, and I wavered on my feet.

With one hand, I gripped the balcony rail to steady myself. I studied the Tower until something caught my eye. It wasn't the mist soldiers, though. No, my blood thundered at the sight of a powerful fae male on the Tower walls, gilded by the light of the moat, his silver crown gleaming. The wind whipped at his cloak, and a few tendrils of fog snaked around him. Strands of pale, blond hair lifted in the breeze.

My blood warmed, cheeks heating at the sight of him. He was all right.

Ruadan. I'm going to see you soon.

I clutched the balcony rail so hard I was at risk of breaking it.

But as I stared at Ruadan across the stony courtyard, the shadows seemed to consume him—a midnight darkness flecked with stars, tinged with moonlight. For a moment, he looked like a god of night, as if he'd been sewn from a starry cloth. Then, he just disappeared into the darkness as if he'd never been there at all.

My heart was beating out of control, and I wondered if I'd just hallucinated him. In the tiny iron box where Baleros had kept me—those times I'd angered him—I'd had plenty of hallucinations. Sometimes I even thought I'd gotten out.

And now that I'd been avoiding dreams, maybe they were creeping into my waking life.

At last, the distinct silhouettes of soldiers became clearer in the misty courtyard below us. My body vibrated with tension. Was one of them holding a note?

"Arianna," said Ciara.

The name irritated me. I wasn't Arianna—not anymore. The death fluttering in my chest did not belong to an Arianna. Arianna lived in a cage and scrambled over the

15

floor for sweets. She was nearly as pathetic as Jared in his plastic ears.

Liora was vengeance incarnate.

With my free hand, I still gripped the balcony rail. My shoulder blades began to tingle, wings ready to erupt. "My name is Liora."

"Liora," Ciara corrected herself from behind me. "Sometimes you can be a bit … intense about things. I think this might be one of those times. I can kind of see it in the way you look like you're about to break the railing."

"What?"

She rose from the sofa. "Look, I sense something bad coming up. My Aunt Starlene always told me that I had a knack for predicting the future. She once put a rattlesnake in her pants when someone offered her five dollars, and I *said* it would end badly because I just had like a sick sense about it—"

"Sixth sense. But not now, Ciara. I need silence."

"Her swelling never went down," she continued. "So as you can see, I was right. And my point is, when you get this message back, I don't want you doing anything crazy, because my sick sense tells me something crazy might be the first thing on your agenda."

"Sixth."

"The first thing," she repeated more sternly.

I slid the whiskey back onto the table. "Never mind. Look, the Shadow Fae are dying in there," I said. "Someone in there is going to assassinate Ruadan. They think I'm to blame, and I'm running out of options."

Jared's door opened. Plumes of fog billowed into the room, and my blood pounded as the mist soldiers marched in. Anticipation lit my nerves on fire as one of the soldiers held out the paper to me.

Now, I'd find out what I'd been waiting for.

I'd expected to find a note of some kind. Instead, someone had just marked my own letter with a red X over the words I'd written. It looked like someone had actually just slashed blood over the page. What the hells…?

You know, they could have at least explained:

You're not wanted.

No death angels allowed.

Will probably kill you, k thx bye.

Any of those things would be preferable to this gods-damned silence. Then again, what if the mist soldiers had given the letter right to the traitor? I needed a new plan.

I gripped the paper hard, my emotions roiling.

Then, I whirled. I snatched my bug-out bag off the ground. I rifled through it for my weapons, and I strapped myself with knives—one holstered around each thigh. I jammed my headlamp on my head.

"I mean, this is exactly what I was talking about," said Ciara. "You have a murdery look, and now you're strapping weapons to your body."

I will crawl up the throats of my enemies and steal their final breaths.

Death pounded in my blood, and I willed my mind to calm. I had to keep that monster in its cage, but I could feel it growing stronger, darkness seeping from my pores.

My foes will choke on their own blood. "Maybe I should kill everyone," I muttered.

Had I said that out loud?

Ciara wrinkled her nose. "Or just a nap, maybe, before you do anything rash? I could get you some of those cheesy crackers you like…?"

I snatched the whiskey off the table and flicked on my headlamp. "I'm going to speak to the Grand Master of the Institute."

17

"Now how the hells do you think you're going to get into that Tower?" Ciara chided.

Without replying, I marched past her, into the hall. I was done waiting to find out if Ruadan was okay or not. The walls, the moat of light—they were for lesser beings, not the angel of death.

Not Liora.

CHAPTER 4

*O*n the winding, ancient road, darkness spilled through my veins.

They thought I was a monster, and I wasn't about to prove them right.

With another long sip of whiskey, I grew a little bit bolder. A little thing like a magical moat couldn't keep me out.

I dimmed my headlamp a bit, accidentally sloshing a little whiskey onto my own face. Maybe I'd been drinking a *bit* too fast, but at least the buzz was helping to calm my death angel side. I was no longer thinking things like *the death of mortals feeds my soul.*

Good, good. If I could permanently stay *just* the right amount drunk, I might not lay waste to life on Earth.

As the death drive dissipated, mental images of Ruadan replaced it: the gentle curve of his lips, the way he wrapped his hand around my neck when he kissed me, the spark of hurt in his eyes when I told him nothing could happen between us. I could almost feel the soothing stroke of his magic licking at my throat.

Desire roared in my chest, so fierce my body trembled.

The wind rushed over my skin, and my purple hair whipped into my face.

If you loved someone, you did everything within your power to keep them safe. If I found Ruadan dead when I broke into the Tower, I wasn't sure what I would do. I wasn't sure if anyone would survive my fury—

Another slug of whiskey to calm the monster within. *Take it easy, Liora. Keep the dark angel locked away before she kills the whole world.*

Somewhere under the roaring river of my thoughts, I had a vague sense of losing control. A drowning voice was saying *that the drunk stumbling through the streets with a crooked headlamp and a rage problem might not be living her best life right now.*

Still, I kept walking. I crossed under a bridge, where pigeons and sparrows roosted above me. They stopped cooing as death approached, flapping away, frantic. I had the sense that the grass and dandelions were wilting around me, that I was a toxic thing.

I am ashen skin, the blood in your lungs.

What I needed was a slightly stronger buzz.

All creatures fear me. All life crumbles to dust before me.

I hiccupped, taking another sip.

Across the street, a group of men laughed raucously over their pints. Didn't they know death itself was near?

Watching them, I stumbled, nearly falling before I righted myself again.

"Hello, darling!" It was one of the men across the street— one wearing a white T-shirt with the cross of St. George. "I like your pretty little headlamp. Give us a smile, darling."

I smiled, then added. "How about I engrave a permanent smile on your face with one of my knives?"

"Ooh, she's a feisty one, isn't she? Come on over here, love. I'd like to tussle with you." He seemed to think I was joking about the knives, although they were clearly strapped to my legs, and I was clearly a monster. Idiot. He pointed to his crotch. "Come on. It's not going to suck itself, is it?"

His friends burst into raucous laughter. I understood how this worked. Not about seduction, was it? Just a performance for the benefit of his friends.

Cold fury simmered, burning away my drunken clumsiness.

I held out my hands to either side, a smile curling my lips. "All right, lads. You want a show? I'll give you a show."

The one in the St. George's cross T-shirt stumbled across the street toward me. "That's a good girl. Give us a show, then."

In a flash of an instant, I was by his side. I touched his cheek, letting the death magic spill out of my fingertips, charcoal gray like smoke. Images flickered in my mind: the bare bones of trees, a cathedral of thin stones arching above, the ribs of a spare skeleton.

"When I'm done with you, you human beast, your skin will curl off your body and your guts will blacken and liquefy. Your life has no meaning. After you putrefy, no one will remember your name."

The full force of my anger terrified even me, and I stumbled back from him. *Shit, shit, shit.*

The human gaped at me, fear freezing him.

"Nope," I held up my hands. "Nope, I'm good. I'm in control. No liquefying organs tonight. Everything is *lovely.* Nice to meet you, fine sirs." I jabbed St. George's Cross in the chest. "But do not harass any more women or I really will peel your skin off. Not even joking."

Nausea crept into my gut as I moved away from them. I'd nearly let the death angel take over completely. If it had, I could have hit the Institute with another dose of the Plague. I could have finished them off before I even got to warn them.

C.N. CRAWFORD

My whiskey buzz had grown richer and deeper, and I nearly didn't notice the tingle of magic down my shoulder blades as I walked away from the humans.

Thing was, I needed to let the monster out just a little in order to get into the Tower.

I will rot your food until your cheeks hollow out, and bony fingers stuff your gullet with grass.

Feathered wings erupted from my back in a burst of euphoria. The scent of myrrh enveloped me. In a wave of ecstasy, I lifted into the air.

Ahhh, this is what I was meant for.

The river wind rushed over my skin. My wings were a rhythmic heartbeat as I lifted into the air. I was born for this —flight in the skies. As my angelic form took over, I could only regret all the years I'd spent tethering myself to the earth, living like a caged beast.

What a waste. A goddess locked in a cage.

Kings and beggars, queens and strumpets. All fall at my feet.

Fifty feet in the air, I skimmed over the stony courtyard. I'd nearly reached the Tower gate.

The Tower: forbidding and silent, secrets locked inside. The fortress and its Grand Master were two peas in a pod.

"Two peas in a fucking pod," I yelled at no one. Apparently, I still had a very good whiskey buzz going, even in my angel form.

The Tower's stone walls failed to respond to my comment. Not a flicker of light, not a twitch of a curtain. The golden moat loomed far below. Still flying, I corked the whiskey bottle. There was a bit left, and I didn't want it spilling.

My wings beat the air, lifting me higher. The Shadow Fae hadn't thought about angels when they'd designed their magical moat. They thought we were all gone. Fools. I giggled as I soared higher.

I flew parallel to the magical barrier, feeling it tingle on my skin. I raced up toward the heavens, wind tearing at my hair.

A moat would keep out the demons, yes, but demons couldn't fly as high as angels. We were meant for the heavens, creatures of the celestial realm. Laughter kept bubbling up, and the dark night winds kissed my skin as I raced higher.

Who needed sleep, anyway? I could do this forever, just me and the sky. Up here, I didn't hear Baleros's voice.

When the air began to thin, and the clouds spread out far below me, the power of the barrier seemed to fade. At last, it glimmered away to nothing.

I'd made it above the protections.

I circled over a moment, looking down at the Tower. I couldn't even see it from here, but I was certain I just had to fly straight down.

I angled my wings, then pressed them flat against my back. I dove in a wild free fall. The rush of the flight was burning away some of my whiskey buzz, and my thoughts started to grow slightly clearer.

I'll admit that at this point the plan didn't seem like the *best* of ideas, but I was already committed to it.

I plummeted, swooping lower and lower, diving, exhilarated. Then, when I could see the stone rings of the Tower below me, I spread my wings out to either side, slowing my descent.

I knew what I was up against. If the Shadow Fae were healthy enough to defend the fortress, I was about to face iron arrows. They'd pierce my flesh, knock me out of my flight, and sap my magic.

I knew they'd hurt, but could iron arrows kill me? Iron didn't hurt angels, but it did hurt the fae. And if my life was in danger, I'd have to fight back with my knives. Granted, throwing knives at the knights wouldn't entirely help the legitimacy of my *look, we're all on the same side here* argument.

As I dove lower, I needed to position myself as close as possible to the entrance of the Cailleach Tower. I hoped to find Ruadan there on his throne, although who knew where he was. I wasn't even entirely sure what time of night it was.

Now, I was only a hundred feet above it. Something whooshed past my head. Another shot skimmed my thigh.

Ah. So the Shadow Fae were healthy enough to shoot. In a way, that was good—

Another arrow zipped past me, and adrenaline surged. I altered my flight path a bit, zig-zagging to make myself hard to hit.

Under attack, the worst part of me longed to unleash the full force of my death magic. I wanted to let it burst from my chest like a plume of black smoke.

I was hurtling for the ground, faster and faster, starting to wonder if I could nail the landing. I mean, flying came naturally to me, but *landing?* I had no idea. I'd never done this before. Still, I had to stay laser-focused right now on one thing, one person.

Ruadan.

And oh, gods, the earth is coming for me fast.

BAM. The force of the fall rattled my bones. I landed hard in the tall grasses outside the Cailleach Tower, grunting as I rolled. The Tower's bells tolled, signaling danger. The impact dazed me, and I scrambled to think of my next move.

Hide, Liora. I hunched down, as if that would somehow make the giant black wings inconspicuous.

Nothing to see here, folks. Just the angel of death invading your fortress, drunk as shit.

Another arrow slammed down in the ground by my side, shouts ringing out. Then another, piercing my thigh. This was getting real. The pain ripped through me, sharp as a hot razor. It definitely felt like iron arrows could kill me, angel or not.

I whirled, scanning the battlements. A flicker of movement on one of the Tower walls—a Shadow Fae readying another arrow. My mind whirred with the calculations, my vision suddenly focused. I could disable him before he shot me, not risk another arrow while I ran for the Tower doors.

As he nocked his arrow, I unleashed my knife, and it sped through the air. The blade found its mark right in the Shadow Fae's wrist.

Before another Shadow Fae got the chance, I pivoted and sprinted into the Cailleach Tower. With the arrow in my leg, I stumbled on the stairs. The weight of my wings threw me off a bit, too. I didn't know how to get rid of them, or if I had any control over that at all.

Nausea was still rising in my gut—either from the whiskey or the iron, or the realization that I'd decided to take on an entire fortress of knights who wanted me dead. I had a terrible feeling I could end up puking in the throne room as soon as I saw Ruadan, and I wanted to avoid that as much as possible. I was here to state my case—that I was a rational person with helpful information, and not just a crazy drunk with an arrow in her leg and wings she couldn't control.

At last, I reached the top of the stairs, and I kicked through the oak doors.

There, I found Ruadan, slumped on the throne, his eyes dark and lifeless. Shadows writhed around him. He wasn't moving. In fact, I saw not a single sign of life apart from the movement of his magic.

Panic thundered through my blood. Had the Plague taken the demigod already?

I couldn't breathe.

CHAPTER 5

"*R*uadan?" My voice echoed off the high stone ceiling. I took a nervous step closer.

Even now, his otherworldly beauty stole my breath— the cheekbones sharp as blades, pale hair cascading over powerful shoulders. His stillness sent shivers dancing up my spine.

My legs shook. "Ruadan—"

Something slammed into my back, and pain blazed from the rear of my shoulder. An iron arrow in my back had knocked me forward, hard, onto my hands and knees.

The whiskey bottle shattered, broken glass cutting my palms. Then, my wings retracted into my body. Already, I was growing weaker from the iron. Whatever happened next, I wouldn't be able to put up much of a fight.

I reached for another one of my knives and looked behind me. Aengus was pointing an arrow at me. Blood poured from his wrist, a wound that had been ripped right open. So *that's* who I'd hit with the knife.

Was he the traitor? I had no idea.

Gripping my knife, I glared at him. "What happened to Ruadan?" I rasped. "Did you do this to him?"

Aengus cocked his head. "Do what to him?"

"Why is he slumped over like that?"

"He's fine, since no one threw a knife at him and the Plague hasn't touched him yet." He let out a cough. "Can't say the same for myself."

"Hmm. I would apologize for the knife, but you did shoot me with arrows."

"Oh, did I? How uncouth of me. I guess I was a bit peeved that you poisoned us with death magic and then staged a terrifying armed invasion of the fortress. Next time, I'll use a sword."

"The way you phrase it really puts a negative spin on it, you know that?" The pain from the arrows in my back and thigh shot through my bones.

Aengus towered over me, green eyes boring into me. I couldn't find the slightest hint of warmth in his expression.

"I came here to deliver a message."

An arched eyebrow. "Oh? From your master, Baleros?"

Wanker. "Baleros is not my master. I did not spread the Plague." I didn't trust Aengus right now, and I wanted to speak to no one except Ruadan. If Aengus was the traitor, I didn't want to pass on information to him. "What's wrong with Ruadan?"

Aengus raised the arrow again, ready to shoot. He didn't look like he was going to answer my question.

The gravity of the situation hit me like a fist to the throat. I could report to Aengus or to no one. I was dependent on him.

"I have information," I said. "But it's for Ruadan." I'd intentionally left the traitor bit out of my letter in case it had fallen into the wrong hands. I'd said only that Ruadan faced a threat, and I needed to explain it to him directly.

Aengus narrowed his eyes. His sickly pallor suggested he really did have the Plague. "You're drunk. I thought you'd invade, but I didn't expect you to be drunk. Though, on second thought, I'm not sure why that would surprise me."

"I'm not that drunk. The buzz wore off quite a bit with the second arrow. Why is Ruadan unconscious? You're sure he doesn't have the Plague?"

"Yes. He's the only one unaffected."

My chest unclenched. "So tell me what's wrong with him."

"I'm not telling you anything. I'm deciding at what point I should kill you and how to do it."

"Wait, wait!" I shouted, my voice echoing off the vaulted ceiling. "Did someone put him under a spell or something?"

"No. Ruadan did that to himself, and he's not available to speak to you right now. As you can see." Blood poured from Aengus's wrist onto the stone floor as he aimed his arrow at me. "You have two seconds to pass on your valuable information before I plant an iron arrow in your eye socket. Will it kill you? I'm not sure. It will definitely sting."

My heart was a frightened rabbit. I didn't have a lot of options. And somehow, I didn't believe Aengus was the traitor. He could be an arsehole, but he'd always been completely loyal to Ruadan. He was trying to protect him even now, in his own obnoxious way.

I held up my hands, dropping the knife. "Fine. I'm not the source of the Plague. I tortured Maddan to get information from him. There's a traitor in here. Someone is using the Unholy Grail to spread the Plague, and he's being commanded by Baleros. When the traitor gets the chance, he's going to kill Ruadan." I nodded at the Grand Master. "So whatever is going on with him, you need to assign a guard or several at all times."

"I guard him."

"Good. Keep doing that. And I'm not done. Baleros's plan

is to weaken the Shadow Fae, steal the World Key, and harvest an army of demons from other realms to take over the world. He will thrive as the Plague spreads. He will use the chaos to make the world his own."

Aengus's bowstring was completely taut.

My gaze flicked to Ruadan, who didn't appear to be registering any of this, his eyes empty.

"You need to protect him." I could hardly think clearly with the pain shooting through my limbs. "Someone in here wants him dead, and he looks vulnerable. Tell me what's going on with him."

"No." Aengus loosed his arrow, and it caught me in the chest. I fell hard to the ground, my mind now registering only the pain.

* * *

When I woke, my mouth tasted toxic, and my throat felt like I'd swallowed shards of broken glass. I coughed, and agony shot through my chest. I'd been shot once in the back, in the thigh, and once through the collarbone. The iron from the arrows had seeped into my blood. If I weren't half angel, I'd probably be dead by now.

Someone had been kind enough to pull the arrows out of me before they'd shoved me into the Palatial Room—the tiniest cell in the Tower's dungeons. The air was heavy down here, rich with the scent of decay. And ... piss. My own, in fact, given the dampness of my trousers.

Yep, this was definitely a low point in my life.

I licked my parched lips. For just a moment, I gripped the bars. The brief touch burned my fingers, reminding me that they were made of iron.

"Barry wants a friend!" A nasal, high-pitched voice rose from the darkness and rattled around my skull.

"What the fuck," I muttered under my breath. I couldn't see much in the gloom, but apparently I'd been stuck down here with another prisoner. One with a voice like nails over a chalkboard.

"Barry wants to know your name! One, two, threeeeeeee!" The shrill voice pierced my eardrums, and I clamped my hands over my ears.

Somehow, I could still hear his voice through my palms.

"Barry likes to eat jam off his fingers. One, two, threeeeeeee!"

Shut the fuck up. Shut the fuck up.

I opened my eyes, still keeping my hands pressed over my ears. After a moment, my eyes began to adjust to the dim light. Somewhere to my left, a torch flickered over the dark cells.

The warm light wavered over Barry—a hairy creature crouched in the cell across from me. Rags hung off his thin frame, and he sat hunched over, pawing at the ground. Despite his wretched state, he had a lumen stone glowing around his neck. How did he get *that*? And why didn't he simply shadow-leap out of here if he had a lumen stone? Maybe I could trick him into giving it to me.

He grinned at me, his teeth long and filthy. "Barry likes to sing. One, two, threeeeeeee!" he whined in a voice that penetrated my skull, piercing my very soul.

"Barry!" I shouted. "If you don't shut up, I will have to kill you."

He thrust out his lower lip. "Barry sad."

I leaned forward, grabbing the iron bars. I didn't even care about the pain from the bars any more. "I don't give a fuck if you're sad, Barry. I need quiet. I have been poisoned by iron."

"Liora needs soft hug," he shrieked, the nasal voice curling my toes. "Barry's flesh is soft like a wheel of cheese. One, two, threeeeeeee!"

I cocked my head. How did this wretch know my name?

He glared at me from beneath his enormous eyebrows. He looked like some sort of caveman. What the hells was he?

"Barry," I said. "How do you know my name?"

"Barry eats flesh from sheeps in pies. Barry puts peeled oranges in pants. Barry—" A coughing fit interrupted him. When he recovered, I could hear the rasping in his breathing.

Another plague victim. Good. Maybe he'd be unconscious soon.

"Since you know so much," I began, "can you tell me what happened to the Grand Master?"

"Barry want a friend!"

I gritted my teeth. "I'll be your friend if you give me your necklace."

A look of panic crossed his features, and he tucked it into his shirt. "Barry wants to love you."

I couldn't take this anymore. I was retreating to my happy place. I pressed my shaking palms over my ears once more, doing my best to block out his shrill yammering.

I leaned back against the craggy rocks of the Palatial Room, trying to will myself back to sleep.

CHAPTER 6

I completely failed to sleep, and instead was forced to listen to Barry the Caveman shriek about all the types of food he liked, and reiterate his previously established desire for friendship, hugs, and peeled oranges in his pants. He was worse than the iron wounds eating at my body.

At last, footfalls tapped farther down the hall, then the sound of a coughing fit filled the dank dungeon. Another plague victim coming for us.

Please. Please, I just need anyone else to talk to.

By this point, I had no idea how much time had passed. It felt like about eight years. But in non-Barry measurement, where the time passed normally, it was probably something like six hours.

"Barry likes to feel potatoes! Potatoes have the gentle curves of a woman. One, two, threeeeeeeee!"

Nausea rose in my gut, and I waited eagerly for the new visitor.

To my shock, Barry stood up in the cell across from me. He dusted off his clothes, and he waved. "Oh, heya, Niall."

I blinked. Barry's voice had become completely normal—soft and deep and ordinary-sounding.

"Hi, Barry." Niall—one of the Shadow Fae—crossed into view and carefully handed Barry a thermos through the iron bars.

"Cheers, mate," said Barry, sounding like a perfectly normal person. He took a sip. "Oh, you've sweetened it as well, that's lovely. Two sugars? That's exactly how I like it. You know, I was catching a bit of a chill down here. Bit damp. Not great for the ol' plague symptoms, if I'm honest," he grumbled.

Niall shot me a furious look, and he pointed at me. "We've got her to thank for that."

At this point, I was thoroughly confused. I gaped as one of Barry's eyebrows drooped off his face.

"Whoopsy-daisy." Barry pressed the eyebrow back on again.

He was wearing fake eyebrows?

"Anyone care to tell me what's going on?" I asked.

Niall glared at me. "You infected everyone with the Plague, invaded the Institute, and you will likely be exalted in the morning when the Grand Master gives us permission."

Exalted, unfortunately, was the ancient fae word for a torturous death. Evisceration, if I remembered correctly.

Niall pivoted, walking away. No tea for me, I supposed.

"Wait, Niall. I need to speak to Ruadan." My voice echoed off the stone walls. Niall did not reply.

And then, it was just Barry and me again.

I glanced at him. He leaned against the wall, sipping his tea. He patted his false eyebrow.

"Who are you, and why have you been tormenting me with that shrill voice?" I asked.

"Ahh, well, I am in fact Barry." He coughed again. "Got a bit of the Plague from your death magic, so I'm feeling a little

poorly. I'm a new recruit, hoping to be a Shadow Fae. Apparently, there was an opening since you turned out to be a...."
He scratched his cheek. "Repulsive abomination or whatever they call it."

"They're calling me a *what?*"

"Ruadan, the new Grand Master, disapproved of traditional torture methods, so he asked us to get creative. This what I came up with. I workshopped it for a few days with the other lads. Aengus said you'd end up in here when we caught you, and we should test it out before your execution. It's good, right?"

"You've got to be kidding me." Even with all the iron in my blood, there was a chance I could still kill him and everyone else in the Institute if I wanted to. Only the fact that I cared about the Institute stopped me from trying. "And they already gave you a lumen stone?"

"Guess so. What did you think of the 'one, two, threeeee' bit? Niall wasn't sure—" He cleared his throat. "Sorry, I'm not really supposed to break the fourth wall like this. Do you mind if I just...."

He took a sip of tea, then returned to his crouching position, hunching over and pawing at the dirt.

"Barry pretends his hand belongs to a beautiful woman. One, two, *threeeeee!*"

Death beats in my breast like raven wings. Their bodies will feed the soil.

* * *

ANOTHER SIX HOURS or perhaps four hundred years passed before Aengus arrived, his loud cough heralding his arrival.

"Heya, Aengus," said Barry, cheerfully, dropping character.

"Good work, Barry." Aengus's injured hand had been

bandaged, and he glowered at me. "Did you get any information out of her?"

Barry blinked at him. "I wasn't really … I didn't actually know there was a purpose to this, as it were."

It seemed like ages since I'd had a sip of water, and my mouth was so dry I could hardly wet my lips enough to speak.

"Aengus," I rasped.

He cocked his head and stared down at me. "Your time has come."

My heart sank. "What time has come?"

"The Grand Master has awakened."

This was better news. "Awakened from what?"

"He was communing with the void." Aengus started coughing again and wiped the sweat off his forehead. "This illness you spread is deeply unpleasant. I feel that I am rotting from the inside out."

"It wasn't me, fuckwit." I closed my eyes, marshaling my patience. "You're letting the real threat swan around the Institute. You're not even protecting Ruadan right now, because you're letting Baleros trick you. Look, can you get back to the part about Ruadan communing with the void? What does that mean, and why is he doing that when he clearly has better things to do?"

"Everyone in the Institute wanted you dead, since you're a terrorist and an abomination."

Any icy shard of rage. *Before I kill you, you will watch your own teeth rot and fall from your mouth like October leaves. Your blood will spatter on your porcelain sink.*

I slowed my breathing, trying to behave like a normal fae. "I do not feel that *abomination* is an accurate description of my nature."

Or did I?

"You know what?" Aengus shot back. "I don't actually feel the need to explain this to you. You're coming with me now."

"Care to share where we're going?"

"Not particularly," said Aengus. He unlocked the iron bars, and the door creaked open. With all the iron in my blood, I couldn't make a break for it even if I'd wanted to.

I gripped the jagged rocks, trying to pull myself up, but my body was weak from the iron poisoning. Halfway up, I grew dizzy and fell back into the rough walls. Then, with an iron will, I righted myself.

As I stepped into the hall, Aengus gripped me hard by the elbow, yanking me out. The sudden movement stirred a wave of nausea, and I turned away from him to vomit back into the Palatial Room. From the burning, I was pretty sure it was mostly the whiskey from the day before. I wiped a shaking hand across my mouth.

If things went really poorly, I'd probably be executed in a horrific manner. If things went well, I'd probably end up sitting in that pile of my vomit. That was a *best*-case scenario.

"Are you quite finished?" asked Aengus.

I straightened as best I could, then leaned into him. "I'm realizing, now, I made a mistake when I aimed in the other direction."

"You smell disgusting," he said.

I smiled at him, pleased he had to deal with my stench. "Do I offend your delicate sensibilities? At one point, I thought you were a warrior. Silly me. You really ought to leave here and form a knitting club."

"Are you scared of dying?" asked Aengus.

A flash of fury lit me up, the death angel straining on her tether. "I want you to know I'm acting with a great deal of restraint right now, Aengus."

Choke on bile.

Aengus's sallow cheeks paled even further.

I'd known the risks when I'd come in here, that I'd probably be hit with arrows. I'd never imagined that Ruadan would allow my death.

Of all the things Ruadan could have been doing—fortifying the castle, finding Baleros—instead, he'd spent these weeks floating around in the shadow void?

When you loved someone, you did anything in your power to save them. Meanwhile, he'd slipped off to the shadow void.

Betrayal pressed down hard on my broken body. "Killing me won't solve your problem. Baleros is coming for Ruadan whether I'm here or not."

We reached the top of the stairs, and Aengus unlocked another iron gate. When he pushed through the next set of doors into a hall, sunlight streaming through the peaked windows blinded me. So, it was daytime.

Wincing, I held up a hand to shield my eyes. A wave of dizziness washed over me, and I leaned into Aengus again while darkness claimed my mind.

CHAPTER 7

a shock of cold woke me—icy water trickling down my hair, my shoulders.

I lay flat on my back on the flagstones, staring up at Aengus and Niall. Barry stood just behind them, one of his false eyebrows drooping.

"There," said Aengus. "She's awake again. Pity the ice water didn't wash the stench away."

He held out his hand to help me up, but at this point, I'd walk on my own two feet if it killed me.

With a great deal of effort, I forced myself up onto my elbows. Grimacing, I rolled to my side, then pushed myself up to a sitting position. On shaking legs, I stood slowly.

When I'd straightened as much as I could, I felt magic whispering down my shoulder blades.

I shot a ferocious look to Aengus. *Cross me, fae, and your body will wither and rot like a blighted plant.* I stared into his bloodshot eyes, and the urge to unleash death nearly overwhelmed me.

Shaking, I turned from him to face the throne room.

When I hobbled into the hall, I tuned out everything else

except Ruadan before me. I forgot about my filthy appearance, the piss on my trousers, the fake caveman trailing behind me. I forgot how much I hated Aengus, and the pain wracking my body. I barely registered the other Shadow Fae lined up in the hall on either side of me, gaping at me.

My eyes were locked only on Ruadan, and his on mine. His piney scent hit me, tinged with apples. And for that moment, the death angel drifted away from me.

Ruadan looked as electrified as I felt. He straightened when he saw me, his entire body tense. Darkness swirled in his eyes, and shadows writhed in the air around him. As our gazes met, the temperature in the room plummeted about twenty degrees. The flames on top of the torches wavered in the blast of cold air, some of them snuffing out.

My gaze swept over him, taking in his powerful body, the thickly corded muscles and savage tattoos that covered his forearms—the silver crown that gleamed on his head. He was a vision of pure, dark power. Aengus had been right. The Plague hadn't touched him.

I may not have looked like it from the outside, but a dark power lived within me, too—my own destructive monster, tethered in its cage. They'd threatened to eviscerate me. I should be unleashing that power now, letting it tear through every living creature in here. But some primal, instinctive power compelled me to protect Ruadan, even now.

Was it the same for him? As he stared at me, he gripped the arms of his throne so tight it looked like he could crack the stone, his obsidian eyes piercing me.

In his view, I was a threat to the Institute. I'd infected them and taken their mist army. Logic dictated that I needed to die for the good of the Shadow Fae.

Logic also dictated that I should kill all of them before they had the chance.

You will sicken—

A rocky barrier rose in my mind, slamming right into my death thoughts. What was that about?

"Liora," said Ruadan. The sound of my real name on his tongue wrapped around my body like silk. The sensual voice of an incubus, as deadly as his wrath.

"Grand Master Ruadan," I said.

"The Shadow Fae here believe you are part of Baleros's plans to weaken our defenses. They believe you spread the Plague."

I held my breath. If Ruadan lost faith in me, I wouldn't be able to take it. The betrayal would be a sword in my heart.

"You transformed into your angelic form," he went on. "You broke into the Institute, armed."

A coughing fit erupted in the hall, echoing off the high ceiling. I glanced at the other fae around me. Melusine stood huddled against a pillar, her eyes glassy. Apart from Ruadan, demigod that he was, everyone in the room looked sick—pale skin, dry lips, shadows beneath their eyes.

"I broke in here to give you a message," I said. "There is a traitor in here, and he is the one who spread the Plague."

Aengus folded his hands in front of him. "The traitor is obviously you. No one else doubts that, right?"

"It is obvious," said Niall. "And if nothing else, she is a child of the apocalypse. It is our mission to destroy her kind."

"And by the way." Anger laced my voice. "While you were floating in a giant black hole for the past few weeks, we could have been teaming up to kill Baleros. I mean kill him for good."

Ruadan's head tilted back, and he stared at me, challenging.

Aengus stepped into the center of the room. "Let's get back to the execution."

Melusine cleared her throat. "If I may speak? Grand Master? It seems to me that we know the Old Gods chose

Liora. They knew what she was, and they chose her anyway. We saw what happened to Grand Master Savus when he tried to defy their will."

I was pretty sure I heard Aengus mutter something about how the Old Gods were wrong.

Ruadan's dark magic whipped at the air around him. "The Old Gods approve of her. And now, her guilt or innocence will be determined by another of the earthly gods."

Tension crackled in the air.

"Why are we giving her this chance?" Niall protested. "It's obvious she spread the Plague here in the Institute."

"I have been in the void for weeks." Ruadan's tone brooked no argument. "This is what Nyxobas has instructed me to do. He will put her on trial in the void. As you know, he does not lie. He will inhabit my body, and we will hear from Nyxobas directly. After all, it is not for us to decide. It is for the gods to decide. Do any of you have any further arguments?"

Cold silence filled the room, and Ruadan's gaze slid over all the Shadow Fae.

Before anyone could utter another word, the room started to change, darkening. A shadowy form rose up behind Ruadan, looming over the hall, silvery eyes burning like stars. Horns loomed above his head in a crescent shape.

I shivered at the vision of the god of night. His presence was dizzying, and I felt like I was standing on the edge of a precipice. I stared ahead of me as the shadow god slipped into Ruadan's body. Star-tinged darkness shimmered around him, and his eyes blazed with silver starlight. Ruadan's tattoos began snaking over his powerful forearms, resembling living creatures.

Dread trembled over my skin. Imbued with the essence of Nyxobas, shadows breathed around Ruadan, and he loomed over the hall.

I felt tiny before him. Broken, too.

A glacial coldness took over the room. I shivered, hugging myself. Was the trial beginning already? I wasn't ready.

The voice that Ruadan used to speak was not his own, but seemed to come from the iciest depths of Hell. "Chaos reigns in the Institute."

His pale gaze fell on me. Despite my primal instinct to flee from an earthly god, I forced myself to stay still. Looking at a god was like facing a wild animal. If I showed fear, he'd eat me alive. With an iron will, I straightened my spine.

"Half angel," said Nyxobas. "Celestial harbinger of death. Half fae, of the Old Gods. Her presence here sows discord. A traitor lives among you, spreading plague. Only a death angel can fix it. Did the deathling cause this, or another? Each of you will prove your loyalty by leaping into the void. In the vast shadows, you will prove your purity. Once I have found the traitor, the portal will seal over."

The shadows faded around Ruadan, and the godlike enormity slipped away.

I let out the long breath I'd been holding.

So this was Ruadan's ploy to maintain control within the Institute—bring in the big guns. Almost no one wanted me here, but they wouldn't argue with Nyxobas.

Aengus looked furious. "All of us are to be tested? You know the risks of leaping into the void."

I didn't, as it happened. "What are they, exactly?"

Melusine raised her hand and immediately began speaking. "I know this one. Time can pass differently in the void. And if you spend too long there, you will return as a demon."

Ruadan still gripped the armrests of his throne. "Nyxobas's decision is clear. You all go into the shadow hell. Succeed, and you join us again. Fail, and it means you are a traitor to the Institute. Nyxobas will seal the portal and claim your soul."

So *that's* what Nyxobas got out of this. The man loved claiming souls.

I stared at the Grand Master, shadows still pooling in his eyes. Was this all an elaborate way of getting me off the Institute's kill list?

"Grand Master—" Aengus began.

One withering look from Ruadan silenced him. "You are all dismissed. All of you apart from Liora."

Around me, the other Shadow Fae turned and began marching out of the room. Fury etched their features, and at least two of them made rude gestures at me.

When they'd all left, the heavy oak door closed behind them, leaving me alone with the Grand Master.

He rose from his throne and crossed to me, moving swiftly. "Your attack on the Tower was not a good idea."

"It wasn't an attack. I was trying to speak to you about the traitor's threat." My mouth and throat felt like sandpaper.

Ruadan scooped me up as if I weighed no more than a sparrow, and I leaned into his chest. I closed my eyes, listening to his heart as he carried me.

"Why did you slip away to the void for weeks? We could have been doing something more useful, like teaming up to kill Baleros."

He held me tight, walking with me in his arms. "I killed him before I went into the void. I hunted him down and sliced Emerazel's sigil off his body. Then I cut off his head."

I opened my eyes, my heart leaping. "You did? So he's dead?"

His features darkened. "Cutting off the sigil didn't work like we thought it would. He returned. Emerazel brought him back."

Nausea curdled my stomach. "You mean we can't kill him?"

"Everything can be killed. I just don't know how, yet."

I leaned into his chest again as he carried me down the stairs. "Where exactly are we going?"

"To fix you before your trial. Nyxobas could return at any point, but I don't want you going into the shadow hell broken like this." His seductive voice held an edge I couldn't ignore.

Already, his soothing magic was whispering over me.

"Speaking of running out of time, we need to keep you safe. Baleros's agent could attack at any moment."

"Shhh," he said. His grasp on me was impossibly gentle, like he was afraid of breaking me.

And yet, when I looked up at his face, I could see a cold, hard rage written there, and the Wraith's perfect features blazed with the ancient wrath of an unforgiving god.

CHAPTER 8

*R*uadan lay me gently by his burbling stone bath. Outside, the sun was setting, and vibrant pumpkin rays streamed through the warped window glass. The light washed over the beautiful planes of Ruadan's face, giving him a warmth that contrasted with his cold expression.

I couldn't feel the pain in my chest anymore, but I felt weak as a withering dandelion.

I blinked, trying to focus. The iron was not only messing with my body, but it had started to screw with my mind, too.

"I'm going to undress you."

"Fine." My mouth tasted like a dry riverbed, and clouds had gathered in my mind. "Wait, why?"

"The water will help to clean your wounds, and the angelica and lavender in the bath will help me to heal you. They will slow the spread of the iron in your system while I pull it out with my healing magic."

Someone had turned my throat into gravel. "I need something to drink."

I lay against the stony bath while Ruadan crossed back into his room. He returned a moment later with a tall glass of water. I took it from him and drank it down. Water had never tasted so delicious and pure before.

While I slaked my thirst, Ruadan crouched by my side. I put the glass down on the stone, and nodded at Ruadan, signaling that I was ready for him to undress me. I probably could have managed it myself, but I didn't want to move any more than I absolutely had to.

Ruadan reached for me, and he unbuttoned the top of my dress, fingers brushing against my skin. Powerful, cold anger rippled off him. Given how gentle his movements were, his rage didn't fit.

When I looked at him this closely, I saw the full force of it —the angry set of his jaw, the eyes black as gleaming jet. Icy mist clouded the air, and a frigid breeze rushed over the stone floor. For a moment, I almost wondered if Nyxobas had returned. But no—it was just Ruadan, furious as hells.

Why was he so mad at me?

My own fury started simmering. We should be on the same side, but he was rejecting me just because I'd had the misfortune to be born as a death angel. When it came down to it, I had been loyal to him. When I'd unleashed the death angel, I'd been trying to save him. Did he not care about that?

He was still unbuttoning my dress, and my helplessness before him only added to my anger.

I sort of wanted to punch him in the jaw and tell him to piss off with his trial. I'd make a speech on my way out. Something about how we are defined by our actions and not our births, and anyway he was a heartbreaking monster, too, so who was he to judge.

I narrowed my eyes at him, still working on my speech. *Oh, and by the way, Breaker of Hearts, I'm sorry your brothers died, but you ruined my life, too, when you invaded that day, and don't fuck with death angels if you don't want people to die. That's how it works.*

Still, I thought maybe it was better to wait until after he'd healed me before I launched into it. Like, it might be more effective when I could stand independently.

He'd unbuttoned my dress down to my navel, his eyes deeply intent on my wounds. Each one of his muscles was tightly bound, and he looked like a coiled animal ready to strike.

Anger rippled through me, so hot I was pretty sure I snarled. He'd come into my world and ripped it apart. If he'd never come, I wouldn't have killed everyone in the first place.

I will scatter your ashes to the—

A barrier of black rock slammed into my mind. Then, an acrid wave of nausea rose in my gut, interrupting my thought.

I was starting to understand. When it came to Ruadan, my death instinct felt as wrong as the iron in my blood. Deep inside, my death magic warred with an insane, animal sense of protectiveness over him.

Why had I taken arrows for him to get in here? What the hells was wrong with me?

I let out a long breath, then closed my eyes. Mentally, I was drifting. Ruadan had ruined my old life, and right now, it was coming back to me so vividly. I hardly ever allowed myself to think of Eden, because when I did, a sharp tendril of pain curled through me. Now, visions of my home burbled into my mind like spring water: swimming in the clear creek with my mum, the tiny gemstones gleaming in her forehead. My dad used to call me Bug. I couldn't remember why. I think it had started as Lovebug and just got shortened. Once, he'd engraved my nickname on the mantle over the hearth, then etched a crescent moon around it.

"Are you still with me?" asked Ruadan. His healing magic was already starting to brush over my body.

"Yup," I said, but my mind was still in Eden.

I opened my eyes again, meeting his furious, dark gaze with my own anger.

"So," I began. "You feed off heartbreak. How's that going?"

Right now, he was probably feasting off me. He paused his hands by my navel and stared into my eyes. His own eyes were pure black, and I could read nothing in them except wrath.

Ruadan, breaker of hearts, ruiner of lives.

"That's right, lover boy," I crooned. I smiled at him, even though I'm sure there was no joy in it. "We both have our monstrous secrets, and I know yours."

He didn't know I'd been in on that secret, and he went completely still. His healing magic ebbed.

With all the strength I had in me, I leaned forward. "How many hearts have you broken over the centuries? Thousands, I'd imagine. A man looking as nice as you, with those muscles and that perfect face. It must come naturally to an incubus and a fomoire. An incubus stirs up lust. You get people to love you. And a fomoire like you can just drink up their pain."

It enraged me that he could feel *my* heartbreak, and that it was strengthening him right now. If I'd had the energy, I would have smashed everything in the room.

Ruadan didn't answer me, because of course he didn't. Still, I felt the temperature drop even further, until the flag-stones beneath me were blocks of ice. An eternity of silence and frost passed between us.

His eyes were on mine—pure and cold as an arctic night

sky. To my surprise, he leaned even closer, his face close to mine. He pressed his hands on either side of my hips, so close I could practically kiss him.

"You're hurt that I didn't protect you," he said.

"What?" I stared at him. "That is not at all what's happening."

"I failed to protect you."

I blinked. He felt my heartbreak, but he'd completely misunderstood it. "That is not even close, Ruadan. I don't need your protection. I'm hurt that you left me—twice. Once at Hampton Court Palace, and then again for the past several weeks. You abandoned me when you found out what I was."

His face brushed softly against my cheek. "You should have trusted me." His voice—soft as silk, but edged with a sharp blade underneath. "You kept your true nature from me because you feared me."

"You kept yours from me."

"Not because I thought you would kill me for it. You should have known I wouldn't kill you, after everything we went through together."

My heart twisted, anger still roiling. "I was on your kill list for years. My dad is on your kill list. I slaughtered your brothers." The room was frigid, and I started shivering. Ruadan's anger was always palpable. "You're angry that I couldn't read your soul. You feel that I should understand you implicitly without you ever having to speak. My powers are amazing, but that's not one of them."

Ruadan pulled my bloodied dress off my shoulders, his fingertips brushing my skin. I stank like the bottom of a sewer, but it didn't seem to register with him.

"Just to be clear," I said, "I'm not on your kill list?"

His fierce expression made me catch my breath. "Of course you're not. You should never have doubted me. I protect those I love. What sort of a person do you think I am?" His gaze flicked to the festering wound at my shoulder, and he winced. Ice shot through the air. "At least, I try to protect those I love."

And at those words, a buried ember ignited in my heart.

CHAPTER 9

*R*uadan might be Prince of Emain, Grand Master of the Institute, but he had a primitive side. Love meant protection to him. The fact that I'd doubted him had made him feel like he'd failed me. And the fact that I'd shown up in his throne room ravaged by iron wounds made him feel like a failure again.

I was usually really good at being strong and holding my feelings back, but the second I felt safe with someone, the tears would start to flow. And right now, they were stinging my eyes, making my vision even blurry. It was enraging, because I wasn't done being mad.

A tear spilled down my cheek, infuriating me. I wiped it off with the back of my hand. "You should never have come to Eden."

"I know."

"And after we found the Unholy Grail, you left me without saying a word. You looked at me—saw me in my true form—and then just left. Then you came to my room and left me a wreath. You said we needed to get the Unholy Grail together. And after that, you disappeared for weeks. I

51

thought I might be back on the kill list. I had no idea what was happening, because you don't tell me. Your vow of silence made things easy for you, didn't it? You didn't have to speak for all those years. It's a beautiful cop-out. You can avoid communicating with anyone while appearing noble."

He scrubbed his hand over his jaw. "I'm sorry. I'm still out of practice when it comes to talking." The darkness in his eyes faded to violet. "I wanted you here at the Institute, but I couldn't get to you during the past few weeks."

"Why exactly did you disappear into the void?"

"The Shadow Fae were mutinying, with Aengus leading the rebellion. They wanted you dead immediately, and I was worried they'd defy my orders. They agreed to wait to act until we heard from Nyxobas. In order to retain control over the Institute, the Shadow Fae needed to hear from him directly. So I went into the void to contact him. But sometimes time passes strangely there. It felt like just a moment, but I was in the void for weeks." He nodded at the steaming bath. "Can you get in? We need to finish healing you."

I unhooked my bra, letting it fall off me, goosebumps rising over my skin. Then, I grabbed Ruadan's arm. He helped me to stand, and I leaned against his powerful body.

"What happens next?" I asked.

"Nyxobas will arrive when he chooses. He will open the void for you, and you will enter. When you return from the shadow hell, with Nyxobas's approval, you and I are going to find your father. He will help us remove the Plague from the Institute. Then, we find Baleros, and we imprison him forever. You and I, together."

"And you're not going to kill my father?"

"It's no longer my top priority."

"So that's a no, or...?" I winced as I bent over to pull off my knickers, my bones screaming.

"That's a no. We need him."

"Good. So can you make any predictions for when I go through this void?"

"I don't know exactly what will happen." He held onto my arm to help steady me. "Nyxobas isn't particularly communicative."

"Sounds familiar." Then I stepped into the bath, lowering myself into the warm, bubbling water. Steam curled around me as I slid down. I leaned back in the bath, meeting Ruadan's gaze.

He reached out, stroking my throat, then traced his fingertips around the jagged wound on my collarbone. It had gone black and rotten around the edges—disgusting, really. Deep, purplish blood leaked from the wound, and I grimaced at the sight of broken bone protruding from my skin. The veins around the wound pulsed with dark blood.

As Ruadan touched the healthy skin around it, his magic slipped over my body like a balm. With his magic intensifying, the purple in my veins began to fade, the pain ebbing. Deep relaxation spread through my body, and my eyes started to drift closed again. I had absolutely no desire to go into the void. I wanted to stay here forever.

Another memory rose in my mind—this one more recent. I was in the forest, handing Ruadan the crown he'd made for me. A brief look of hurt flashed in his eyes.

A sigh escaped me. "I'm sorry I gave the crown back."

"I'll make you another." His hand moved lower over my ribs, and my skin pulsed with the euphoria of his magic. Already, my body was stirring with arousal at his touch. I breathed in the scent of the herbs in the bath, the air heavy with their perfume.

When I opened my eyes again to look down at my collarbone, I was stunned to find that it had almost completely healed. The skin had closed over, and it looked like a pale, indented scar.

Ruadan's violet eyes never left my face, his expression so intent it looked like he wanted to devour me. Sometimes when I looked at him, the sheer power of him hit me like a gale-force wind.

"Why exactly were you so angry with me when I first came into the Institute?" I asked. "Was it because I'd invaded or because I'd hidden what I really was from you?"

Apart from the hand brushing over my body, most of Ruadan had gone completely still—a strange silence found only among the ancient fae. "I wasn't angry with you." His soft voice caressed my naked skin, a dark temptation. "I was angry with myself, because my men threw you in the prisons."

I arched an eyebrow. "You need to stop thinking that you have to protect me." The arrogance on this one. Darkness roiled between my ribs. I needed no protector. The corner of my mouth twitched anyway. I liked his sentiment, even if it made no sense. "I'm an angel of death. I don't need protecting."

"Well, maybe the other Shadow Fae will pay."

"Pay? How?"

He traced a fingertip lazily in the burbling bath, his magic washing over me, doing its healing work. "Sometimes, in the shadow void, Nyxobas punishes spirits by forcing them to confront the wrongs they've committed on earth. Sometimes to relive them. He forces you to confront your past."

I paled. "And you're sending me into the shadow void."

"Right."

"I have killed *hundreds* of people in the arena, and I slaughtered my entire village. So … it might not be a good time for me there."

"It might not happen for you."

"Good."

I leaned back in the bath. It was then that I realized that

not only was his magic healing my body, it was actually making me feel rested. I'd barely slept in weeks, and yet I no longer felt quite as insane. I was starting to feel … energetic. Gods bless Ruadan and his magic.

As I sucked in a deep breath, the curves of my breasts floated above the steamy water's surface. Ruadan's gaze dipped to them, and his shadowy magic lashed the air around him.

I grabbed a bar of soap from the rocky bath's edge and started to lather myself up, watching his eyes follow my hand's movements. I made the strokes slow and sensual, moving over the tops of my breasts. His desire licked the air around him. Mesmerized, he wrapped one of his hands over mine, lacing my fingers with his. His hand slid over my skin with mine. Heat raced through my body.

A drop of water slid down my throat, and he followed it with his eyes. Then, one of his hands moved away from mine. His fingers brushed down the front of my chest and my waist, and molten heat rushed through my core. An ache began to build in me at his light touch.

It wasn't just his beauty or his touch that stoked my heat. It was knowing that he loved me.

His violet eyes were locked on me, and he began tracing slow circles, moving lower—now in the hollow of my hips. Tingling heat radiated out from his touch. His incubus side was coming out, and he was toying with me.

He drank me in with his gaze, and the look he was giving me promised pure, sensual pleasure. My thighs clenched.

"I know it doesn't make sense to protect you," he said. "It's my instinct, as powerful as my will to live. I want to keep you safe and close by my side."

I wanted to grow claws and sink them into his skin to bind him close to me. I had the same primal instinct to keep him safe—not free from hurt, because he could take a little pain, just like I could. But I wanted to keep him close to me.

My chest flushed, pulse racing. This close to his savage beauty, it was hard to think straight. I only knew I wanted to feel his tongue on my neck, his hands on my breasts, his mouth between my thighs.

As he traced circles over my hip bones, my knees started to fall open, and my breath hitched. Liquid heat flowed through me, and a hot, pulsing ache pounded between my thighs.

I straightened, and my nipples floated just above the warm water. They hardened in the cool air. "You want me close by your side?"

His eyes seared me for a moment, then he leaned closer. "By my side, in my bed," he whispered, his breath warming the shell of my ear. "Naked and wrapped around me forever."

His fingers went to the inside of my left thigh. Despite the heat of the bath, I shivered. I wanted to feel his hand all the way down at the apex of my thighs, but he was moving with the infuriating slowness of an incubus, enjoying his control. He traced light circles on my inner thigh with his fingertips. I shuddered with desire.

I opened my legs wider, desperately aching for him. I wanted him inside me now. "Are you going to come in here?" I didn't like the way it had come out as a desperate plea.

His magic thrummed over my skin, fingers moving just a little higher. With his other hand, he brushed his thumb over my lips. I caught his thumb in my mouth, and I rolled my tongue over it. Now, I burned for him so deeply I could almost moan. In fact, I think I *did* moan.

A low, animal growl rose from Ruadan's throat. I moved my hips until I was grinding myself against his hand. I still needed more.

"Come in here with me," I said in something between a command and a plea.

His fingertips were still teasing me, stoking my lust to an insane ache. A slow smile curved his beautiful lips. "I won't fit, will I?"

Wild hunger blazed in my body. "We'll make you fit."

He dipped his fingers into me, and I writhed against him. *More, more.* That sharp, pounding desire built inside me, until I could think of nothing else but the word *more.*

Dark heat enveloped me. I moved against him, desperate for release. At last, I managed, "Get into the bath with me. Now. No more arguing."

He rose and pulled off his black shirt, exposing his muscled body. He was pure perfection, built like a god. Which made sense, since he *was* part god.

And I was about to have my fill of him.

CHAPTER 10

My gaze roamed over every inch of him. My stomach swooped at the network of tattoos on his body, snaking savagely over his powerful warrior's thighs. As I stared at him hungrily, I almost didn't realize that my own hand had found its way between my thighs to replace his. My breath raced.

At last, he stepped into the bath and kneeled between my legs. He leaned against me. "I'm going to keep you close to me. You're a death angel, but you're *my* death angel, and I keep you safe from now on."

"Then you're my fomoire monster." I wrapped my arms around his neck.

He kissed me sensually, his tongue sliding against mine. Another growl from Ruadan, and his hand gripped my hair, his body stiffening. The slow sensuality was now transformed into raw animal desire. He pulled me hard against him. He was done teasing me now, burning from hunger like I was, claiming my mouth with his wild kiss. I wrapped my legs around him.

Then, with one savage stroke, he buried himself inside me. I gasped, waves of pleasure lighting me up.

There was nothing now except me and Ruadan, and the heat of our bodies merging deeper with each glorious stroke.

Pleasure washed over me, wild ecstasy where our bodies joined. I could only feel the movement of our slick skin together, my tongue on his neck, teeth in his throat. I ran my fingernails down his back as he thrust deeper. The world around me dimmed, and it was just Ruadan and me.

He whispered into my ear, repeating his promise. "From now on, I keep you safe."

It was those words that sent me over the edge, and my cries echoed off the stone walls.

* * *

WITH DAMP HAIR, I lay on Ruadan's chest in the tub. The warm water burbled around us, steam curling about our bodies. The air around him had darkened with shadows, his magic whipping at the air. He brushed his hand over my neck.

The torch flickered in its sconce, and a chill fell over the room. Then, the hot, burbling water turned glacial.

"Ruadan! Gods below. Stop it."

No sooner were the words out of my mouth than I realized that Ruadan's tattoos had begun sliding all over his body again.

I froze, my heart thumping wildly. So *this* was the moment Nyxobas chose to return and to inhabit his grandson's body. While we were lying naked in a tub together, my legs wrapped around him.

He rose from the bath, his eyes shimmering with silver-tinged starlight. I crossed my legs, and I crossed my arms over my chest.

He looked at me impassively, completely uninterested in my nudity. "The time has come for your trial."

As I stared up at him, I had that strange, dizzying feeling that I was standing on the edge of a precipice, and that I wanted to jump. "Right here?"

He shook his head. "You will complete your trial outside. I've opened a portal in the Tower Green."

"Okay. Sure. So, I'm naked and this is a little awkward." Still, I couldn't stay in the freezing bath any longer. "Is there a towel you could hand me?"

A vortex of shadows whirled around him, and his silvery eyes transfixed me. He did not answer.

Of course he didn't; he was Ruadan's grandfather.

Unable to take the icy bath any longer, I stood, my teeth chattering. Maybe it was Nyxobas's complete lack of interest in my nudity, but I quickly stopped feeling self-conscious in front of him.

"Just give me a second to get dressed," I said, plucking Ruadan's shirt off the ground.

"Travelers into my portals may not sully the waters with clothing."

I cast my mind back to the enormous demon named Bael, who'd arrived in the Tower completely naked. He'd said basically the same thing.

"Sure, that makes sense," I muttered. *Weirdo.*

Well, it wasn't like I had my own clean clothes here, and I wasn't going to put the filthy, piss-stinking jersey on again.

"But if we're going outside," I said, "I'm going to at least wrap something around myself. I don't need Barry leering at me."

I strode into Ruadan's bedroom and pulled one of his sheets off the bed. When I turned back to Nyxobas, he'd vanished.

With the sheet wrapped around me, I crossed to the

window. The sun had set completely now, and darkness had fallen over London. The moon seemed startlingly bright, a jewel hanging over the courtyard, and the stars cast silvery light over a transformed courtyard. Where wildflowers had been just moments before was now a gaping chasm, about twenty feet across, filled with dark water.

I swallowed hard as I looked out at it. I was supposed to jump into that abyss, and I had no idea what I'd find when I did.

Ruadan said I'd be facing the sins of my past—but I had too many to count.

* * *

WRAPPED in Ruadan's bed sheet, I stood at the edge of the portal, where the grass and soil simply gave way to dark waters. I had to journey into one of the hells, but at least I felt rested. Sleep deprivation was its own sort of hell, and one that I'd escaped.

Nyxobas—inhabiting my lover's completely naked body —stood nearby, horns gleaming over his head, tattoos slithering around him.

The rest of the Shadow Fae had joined us, wrapped warmly in their cloaks. Fever flushed most of their faces, and beads of sweat dotted their brows. I had to get this over with as fast as possible so we could find my father. It was the only way to heal them all. What did they plan to do if I turned out to be the traitor, as they imagined? They thought they could petition for my father's help after they threw me into the shadow hell? Aengus and the others hadn't thought this through at all.

If the portal sealed over me, it would at least relieve them from a harrowing trial in the shadow hell. Sick as they were, I couldn't imagine they wanted to jump into freezing waters to face possible torture. But didn't they realize they needed my help to rid themselves of the death magic? Right now, they could hardly see beyond their own misery.

I stared into the portal, dreading my own imminent trial. In my heart, fear twined with an insane desire to leap in.

Aengus cleared his throat, then gestured to urge me on. The movement was interrupted by a coughing fit.

I glanced at Nyxobas, who looked like some sort of combination of Ruadan and the god of night—Ruadan with paler skin, darker hair, and phantom horns. He loomed over the edge of the portal, tattoos slithering over his powerful body. He looked beautiful and remote at the same time— strangely alluring despite his otherworldliness. This time, when I looked down at the waters, the urge to jump in was overwhelming.

And this was the essence of shadow magic, wasn't it? The shadow creatures: vampires, incubi, succubi, fomoires of heartbreak…. These creatures possessed the kind of magic that lured and seduced you to your own death.

I took a step closer to the portal, nearly ready to drop the sheet when I remembered everyone was looking on.

I shot Aengus a sharp look. "Turn around. All of you."

Aengus nodded at the other Shadow Fae. Melusine gave me an encouraging nod before she turned away.

As the rest of the Shadow Fae turned away from me, I stared into Nyxobas's silvery eyes. I took one long breath, steadying myself.

Then, I leapt into the portal—but I didn't hit the water. Instead, I plummeted farther down, dropping into pure darkness. My arms lifted above my head, cold air racing over my bare skin.

Then, I could no longer feel my body at all. It was just me and the darkness. I had no sense of up or down, no sense of horizon. Had I ever existed at all?

Emptiness began to poison my thoughts. If I'd never been alive, then I'd never loved…. It had always been this way—just me and the darkness.

No, no. Had I been alive once?

It didn't matter. I wasn't alive now. I didn't exist now. And now was all that mattered.

Wisps and fragments of thoughts floated in the wind like dandelion seeds.

Love dies when we die….

I never loved.

The pain of this thought hit me so intensely I was sure my mind would shatter, and the portal would close me inside forever.

CHAPTER 11

*I*t was at that point that a new thought struck me. I could feel pain.

I could feel. If I could feel, it meant I existed.

I exist.

Feeling started to return to my body, to my limbs and my fingertips and the tips of my toes. I touched my own throat, my fingers warm against my skin.

"I exist," I said out loud, the sound of my own voice a strange and illicit thrill, vibrations rumbling against my hand. A stony floor materialized beneath my feet, and I sighed with relief at the feeling of stability. Something solid underneath me.

Then, a thin, silver light, like the light of the stars, washed over the space around me.

I wasn't naked anymore. I'd been dressed in a long, silvery gown, the fabric pure gossamer. My purple hair cascaded over bare shoulders.

I wasn't wearing shoes. As I walked forward, a world began to take shape around me, the contours oddly familiar.

A gray cottage of rough-hewn wood, a narrow village road. Buildings wrapped in flowering vines.

Just on the edge of the village, beyond this clearing, dark forests yawned on either side. I didn't want to look into those woods.... It wasn't safe there. They'd always seemed so alive to me, the trees breathing and moving, but now their trunks stood like stone sentinels ready to kill me.

It was only safe here, in civilization. The darkness in the forests was just a little *too* dark, too savage.

Why was it so empty here?

It took me a little while to realize what I was looking at. Then, the shock of familiarity hit me.

This was Eden—where I'd lived with my mum and dad long ago, before Ruadan had come. This was the village they'd created—the wooden homes, the elaborate stone temples, overgrown with honeysuckle and moonflowers. The perfect melding of the wild and the divine. This beautiful world was the only one I'd known in those days, before I'd leapt through the portal to London.

Sadness pierced me as I was forced to face the truth.

I'd killed all of them, hadn't I? And this was my reckoning.

That's why the buildings were empty. Gods, I just wanted to see another living person, someone with a beating heart. Here, the loneliness was crushing.

The sound of footfalls pattered behind me, and I whirled.

"Hello?" I called out.

Silence greeted me. I exhaled, walking again.

I wasn't sure I wanted to see my old house, the one where my mum had tried to teach me to dance, where my dad had read me books in his lap. I didn't want to see it empty and dead like these buildings. These were the carcasses of my past life.

Footfalls again, and I turned. This time I caught a flash of pale skin, a glimpse of purple—

My heartbeat raced. "Hello?"

Whoever it was had disappeared around the corner of a house, and I picked up my pace to follow.

"Who's there?" I needed to find them. I couldn't be alone here.

When I rounded the next corner, I saw her—the little girl with the amber eyes; the short, purple hair that she'd cut herself. A white dress short enough to show off her skinned, dirty knees. Her mother had wanted her to wear it. She hated dresses, the way you were supposed to keep them clean and unwrinkled, and she wanted to run through the woods and pretend to hunt.

I swallowed hard. "Liora," I whispered.

She giggled, then ran off into the gloom of the forest.

"Wait!"

I chased after her, my bare feet pounding the dirt. How could a little girl run so fast? My blood turned cold as I ran deeper into the forest. Blossoming hawthorn trees surrounded us, but their branches looked oddly sharp and spiked—half tree, half medieval weapon.

She ran on the narrow path, and I tried to keep up with her. The branches scraped my skin, drawing blood like claws.

My pulse pounded in my ears. I had to chase her. I had to tell her to be careful—that a fae cohort would come here today. A fomoire would ruin her world, and she had to be ready. I broke into a sprint.

How the hells was she so fast?

"Stop!" I yelled.

Abruptly, the little girl stopped and turned to see me.

She gaped at me, her eyes black and empty. "You don't exist. You never did. You never loved."

My legs started shaking, and I felt the ground giving way beneath my feet again. A seed of understanding began to bloom in my mind. "I'm onto you." I gritted my teeth.

"You're not a little girl. You're not me. You're a demon of the void."

At my words, her body began to shift, limbs elongating. A tall, pale demon appeared before me.

No longer a little girl, the demon loomed over me. Silver horns jutted out from his blond hair, and his canines glinted. He wore a blue T-shirt and jeans, which seemed a bit weird for a demon.

"Liora," he chanted in a singsong voice. "Liora. Liora, Liora. Death poisons her aura."

Anger tightened my lungs, my fists clenching. As he sang, that old image rose in my mind—the one of my mum lying flat on her back, the skin around her neck discolored to a bruise purple.

The demon's form flickered away again. "She killed her mum, she killed her friends, and they won't come back anymore-a."

Rage ignited, and I ripped a spiked branch off a tree. "That doesn't even rhyme properly, you stupid twat!" I shrieked.

"Liora, Liora...." He continued on with his enraging chant. He kept flickering between the tree trunks—just glimpses of his tall, pale body.

This was a trial, wasn't it? That meant I probably had to kill him. Good. I *really* wanted to kill him.

But the more I chased him, the farther away he seemed to slip. The ground looked purple here, discolored and rotten. The color of bruises, of rotting flesh ... blood stained the soil.

If I didn't kill this demon, I'd be trapped here forever, forced to relive my worst memories. Forced to tread on my mother's neck.

That's what Hell was, wasn't it? Nyxobas, you fucker. Was this really necessary?

Baleros's twentieth law of power: Bring your enemy to you.

I stopped in my tracks, closing my eyes, catching my breath.

Silence yawned around me. Then, the icy stroke of the demon's fingertips up my spine sent a sharp pang of loneliness shooting through me.

You never loved....

I spun around, driving the spiked branch right into the demon's heart. His hazel eyes widened with shock. There was something familiar about them.....

Dark blood poured from his chest. Then, he disintegrated like dust, and particles of his demon body floated away on the wind.

I sighed. There. Alone again.

I looked around me, waiting for the portal to open once more. I'd swim out of the portal water and drag Ruadan back to bed before we went off in search of my dad.

But no portal was opening in the earth. Instead, the forest around me began to shift, the sharp lines of the trees growing softer. Then, the godsdamned blond demon appeared again, farther along down the winding forest path. He walked toward me, his smile mocking. I was sure he was about to start singing again.

"How many times do I have to kill you?" I shouted.

I gripped my head, my mind whirling. Maybe I'd approached this wrong. Since joining the Institute, there had been a few trials where I *wasn't* supposed to kill someone. The gorta, the creepy banshee in that East London shop.....

It would be nice if someone would lay out the ground rules ahead of time, given that my first instinct was always to kill.

I let out a long, slow breath, studying the creature before me. The closer I looked, the less it looked like he was mocking me. In fact, his strangely familiar hazel eyes looked haunted. By his pointed ears, I could tell that he wasn't just a demon. He was at least part fae.

"What do I know you from?" I asked.

His mouth opened and closed mutely, and the stricken look on his face filled me with guilt.

Then, he spoke again. "I ... a darkness. I ... a darkness. Dick."

I scratched my cheek. "Okay, friend. What am I supposed to do here?"

"Amgggr pentagra bus hole."

"Yeah, I'm going to need something a little clearer." I scrunched my nose as a seed of understanding began to bloom in my mind. "Did you used to be a fae? Have you been trapped in the demon world, slowly turning into a demon?"

He nodded. "Stank rubs."

"How long have you been here?"

He gripped me hard by the shoulders, his lip trembling. "Eternity."

"Literal eternity or...?"

His fingers tightened even more. "Since you killed me."

I felt the world tilting beneath me, time slowing down. My mouth went dry. "I killed you. In the gladiator ring?"

He stared down at me, the planes of his face growing more familiar.

"Who are you?" I stammered.

"Liora," he whispered, his expression desperate, pleading.

"No. What's your name?"

"Darkness. Mike."

Panic gripped me. Mike—Mike from Eden. The boy I'd chased through the forest.

"What are you doing here?"

"I ... a darkness...."

I swallowed hard. "Right. I killed you."

He nodded, his grip loosening a little on my shoulders.

"Nesting locks of dark. Throglint oak." His eyes went wide, then he whispered in my ear, "Dick."

I swore to the gods that before he'd been in the shadow hells, he'd made sense. This place had warped him completely. Nausea rose in my gut. I'd done this to him. I'd sent him here, and he'd completely lost his mind.

"Okay, Mike. It hasn't been an eternity. More like a decade. I know it feels like an eternity." I frowned. "I want to get you out of here." I looked around the dark wood, searching for a way out. I didn't see one.

Nyxobas hadn't sealed me in here, had he?

"Any clues about how to get out?"

"Infestations demon Tznaia Amman roots, deathling open door. Darkness." He was speaking a pidgin demon language. Gibberish.

Or was it gibberish?

"Please." He kept his hands on my shoulders. "Miracle. Deathling."

Deathling open door.

"Where is the door?" I asked.

"Deathling," he repeated.

The gods of death had dominion over the dead. I could *open* the door.

I'd already seen that my own thoughts could influence the space around me. The less empty I felt, the more power I had. I closed my eyes, thinking of Ruadan and the floral crown he'd given me in Emain. This time, I rewrote the script, imagining that I'd taken the wreath from him. In this version of the story, I put the wreath on my head.

Warmth spread through my chest, and I stepped away from Demented Mike.

When I opened my eyes again, I felt Ruadan's electrifying presence around me, and I smelled the scent of pine. I felt loved.

Then, I willed the ground before me to cleave open. Dark, churning waters rose from the forest soil, and a portal ripped open the forest floor.

I grabbed Demented Mike around the waist, and I pulled him into the water with me.

CHAPTER 12

Catching my breath in the air, I hoisted myself out of the freezing portal. I clawed my way onto the grass, then frantically turned to reach into the cold water for one of Mike's long limbs. I grasped his arm, clutching on tight, and I dragged him out of the portal. He gasped, holding onto the portal's grassy rim. Mike's dark eyes were wide with wonder at the stars above us.

I tried to ignore the fact that I was completely starkers once more, and that all the male Shadow Fae were staring at me right now. I sat on the grass and folded my knees to my chest, wrapping my arms around them.

Aengus frowned at me, folding his arms. "Okay. Okay. So Nyxobas let you back. You're not the traitor. Now, who the hells have you brought back with you? And must you always bring back these wretches from the hell worlds?"

"He's an old and dear friend," I said, conveniently omitting the part about that time I'd killed him and sent him to the shadow hell. I hugged my legs tightly to my chest.

From behind, I felt a sheet wrap around my body, and I

looked up at Ruadan. It was him again, his eyes violet. The god of night had left us for now.

"Well," said Aengus, "that's the first one over."

I glared at him. "Are you going to admit that you were wrong about me being a traitor and that you owe me an apology?"

Aengus rolled his eyes. "Fine." His tone was exasperated. "I'm sorry I said you were a traitor and that we should rip out your entrails in a painful execution. You're still an abomination, though, and I make no apologies for that view." His forehead wrinkled with consternation. "Is it just me, or are the youth of today particularly *sensitive* about things? Snowflakes, the lot of you."

With every interaction, I was starting to grow more certain that Aengus was the traitor. I fought the urge to just push him right into the portal and watch Nyxobas claim his soul.

Barry raised his hand. "Just to clarify, we don't all need to go in, do we? I'm only a recruit, so obviously I'm not a part of this."

"Everyone in the Institute," said Aengus. "Until we find our traitor."

Barry paled. It was, after all, a terrifying prospect to leap into a hell world where we were forced to reckon with past sins. Barry would probably be subject to a torturous Neanderthal routine.

I stood, holding the sheet tight around myself, and started to cross to Ruadan.

But as I took a step toward him, pale light began beaming from his eyes once more, and his tattoos slid over his powerful forearms, his chest, his muscled thighs. I tried not to think about how sexy he looked right now. The world of magic was always strange, but lusting after your lover while his grandfather's spirit inhabited his body crossed some sort of line even for me.

Nyxobas-Ruadan shadow-leapt over to Aengus. The god grasped the knight by his throat and lifted him high in the air. Aengus's clothes burned away from his body, leaving him completely naked.

Then, Nyxobas threw Aengus into the portal. Dark water splashed high into the air, shimmering with flecks of silver.

I stared as the watery surface calmed. Now, the moon and stars shone off its glassy surface.

I glanced at Mike, who was also nude, regretting that I didn't have a sheet for him. Not that he seemed to mind. His hands were on his hips, proud as could be, and he strode through the flowers, whistling.

I looked at the portal again. It didn't seem to be closing over with grass like I'd expected, trapping Aengus inside. I leaned over and skimmed my fingertips along the cold, glassy surface. It was black ice, and as I touched it, steam curled off.

Then, the ice cracked with a booming sound. Another enormous crack, and Aengus's fist broke through the surface. Frantic, he grasped for the edge of the portal with one hand, punching another hole in the ice with the other.

I glanced at Ruadan. Nyxobas still imbued his body, and he seemed unmoved by this struggle. We weren't supposed to help him, were we?

At last, he punched a hole big enough for his head and shoulders. His lips had gone blue, and he gasped for breath. Manically, he clawed and scrambled over the ice, until he flopped, naked, onto the grass.

He curled into the fetal position, hugging his knees to his chest. He was whispering something that sounded like *trapped in the stone room,* the same words over and over again. Then, "Shot through with iron arrows...."

I crossed my arms, looking down at him. I *really* wanted to gloat, but gloating about the misfortunes of someone already dying of the Plague seemed a bit tacky.

Barry gaped at him, pale as milk.

When I looked around at the other Shadow Fae, they looked just as terrified. But they looked ill, too. Most were too weak to stand, and sweat dampened their brows. Melusine's throat bulged with swollen glands, and her eyes were closed.

My throat tightened. Would they survive a brutal trip into the void? Fever and disease were eating them alive.

Ruadan loomed over the portal—no longer filled with Nyxobas's power, but still exuding dark magic. "As you see, Nyxobas has returned both Aengus and Liora. They are not our traitors. The god of night has left us for now, but he will return to test the rest of you when he sees fit. In the meantime, no one leaves the Institute."

Niall's teeth were chattering, and he coughed into his arm. "So what now? We just wait for Nyxobas to return while we die of the Plague?"

I crossed to Ruadan, my bed sheet dragging over the wet grass. "No. Now we find my father, the angel of death, and he's going to cure all of you." I glanced at Ruadan. "But we should probably put some clothes on before I introduce you to my family for the first time."

Melusine rubbed a swollen gland in her neck, wincing as if in pain. "If your father can cure us, why can't you? You're right here."

I shook my head. "I don't know how. My father will."

She coughed. "You could at least try. You have the same powers as your father, and you're right here. What if we have to go through the trials while fever is killing us? Look at Aengus."

Tension vibrated through my body. She simply didn't

understand how badly this could backfire. "I could make it worse. If I try to use my death angel powers, you could end up sicker. Trust me. Look, I promise we'll be back quickly. We just need to get some clothing on, and we will be back within a few minutes with my dad."

So why was it that I didn't quite believe the words coming out of my own mouth?

"Liora is right," said Ruadan. "It won't take long. Asking Liora to experiment with her powers should be a last resort, undertaken only if we cannot find the Horseman or compel him to help us."

Dread crawled up my neck. Why would we not be able to find him? Of course we'd find him. He'd be in Eden where I'd left him.

And yet ... something about my time in the shadow void had seemed like a premonition. Those empty houses, standing like carcasses. Demented Mike had been trapped there. How many others had I consigned to one of the hells?

I locked the cage on my thoughts, refusing to dwell too long on my worst fears.

For the first time in over ten years, Ruadan was going to open a portal to my old home, and I'd see them again. My heart was ready to burst.

I could hardly breathe with the anticipation. When we broke through into Eden, my dad would be waiting for me. He'd pull me into a hug and call me Bug and tell me it wasn't my fault. And that he'd brought my mother back, and that everything was fine.

Then we'd return to London together. As a team—as a family—we'd figure out how to rid the world of Baleros's malignant presence. This would happen.

Right?

I wouldn't let myself think about the nightmarish vision

of my old home in the shadow hell. I refused to entertain the idea that I might find everyone dead. That I'd be standing over a grave for my mum, or that my father had lost his mind. I would definitely not think of him mad with grief, his shoulders slumped, dark wings drooping behind him as everyone he ever loved abandoned him—

My legs felt weak.

"Clothing," I blurted at Ruadan. "We need clothes." I gestured at the Tower walls. "My entire mist army will stay here to guard the Tower. I'll command them to surround the Institute."

Ruadan nodded. "Tell them that if they see anything amiss, they should report to Aengus."

"Yes. Sure. Can we go now?"

I needed to go before the terrifying images claimed my mind. Before I lost my nerve completely.

* * *

IN RUADAN'S ROOM, I pulled a shirt on over my bare chest.

"Are you all right?" Ruadan asked.

"I'm fine. Almost ready."

As if it had traveled with me from the shadow void, sharp emptiness spread between my ribs—a chasm that could eat me alive. I took a deep breath as I slipped into a pair of black leather trousers. My hands shook a bit as I buttoned them.

Fully dressed now, Ruadan closed the distance between us. His healing magic brushed over my skin, soothing my fears. He leaned in and pressed his forehead to mine. Silky magic kissed my skin. "I can go first," he said. "I can see what it's like before you join me."

I closed my eyes, marshaling my resolve. He understood I was afraid of what I'd find there. He'd be returning to the place where he saw his brothers die—but he was thinking of me.

"You can't go alone," I said. "If Adonis is there, you might not make it out alive. If anyone should go alone, it would make more sense for it to be me. I'm the one who can convince him."

Still pressing his forehead against mine, he shook his head *no*. "It's better if I go with you. Eden has been sealed for ten years. I don't know what we will find there."

"I'll be fine. Death angel, remember? I'm very hard to kill."

He straightened. "I don't think that you need me to survive. I just think I should be with you."

I nodded. So maybe he wanted to protect my heart. Maybe he was imagining the same things I was—a landscape of dust and gravestones.

I sucked in a sharp breath. "Mike, the demented fae I brought back, was from my village. I killed him, and he's been in the shadow void this whole time. I think I must have put our whole village in the hells."

Ruadan brushed his knuckles over my shoulder. "He can reverse death magic. He can reverse the Plague. That's why we're going to find him. Maybe that ability was strong enough to bring some of them back. We could be returning to a thriving village in Eden."

My chest unclenched. Ruadan was right. I should not underestimate Adonis. I smiled at him. "Okay. You're right. Let's do this." I glanced at the sword slung around his waist. "Do you really think we should go in armed? It's a family reunion, and it might take a moment for them to recognize me. Going in with weapons might send the wrong message."

"I'll keep it sheathed."

"Fine. And let me walk in front." Then, I pulled on my headlamp. I had no reason to bring the headlamp or the bag, but I just felt better with them. I felt like myself. "Right," I said. "Open the portal before I lose my nerve."

Without another word, the floor opened up in front of us, a watery fissure in the stone that widened.

Ruadan took my hand, his violet gaze on mine. I nodded at him, and we leapt in.

CHAPTER 13

$\mathcal{T}$he freezing vortex pulled us under. I clutched Ruadan's hand as we sank deeper into complete darkness. I found a brief moment of peace in here, a respite of purity in the blackness.

After a few moments, moonlight pierced the water. *Eden.*

I was home. Still holding hands, we started to kick our way to the top. By the time we reached the surface, I felt like my heart was about to explode.

We pulled ourselves out at the same time, and I gaped at the world around me—the dark forest, silvered in the moonlight. The clearing just a hundred feet away. With my head out of the water, I gasped for air. Clutching the portal's mossy edge, I stared at the silent oaks around me. We'd emerged in the woods.

I pulled myself out, and I sloshed onto the rich earth. I breathed in, taking in the smells of moss and ancient trees, the faint aroma of honeysuckle and blackberries—the ones I used to pick with Mike. *Home.*

Ruadan rose, too, and his hand instinctively hovered by

his sword. His muscles were tensed, and he looked ready to kill.

"Simmer down, Ruadan," I said. "It's a family reunion, remember?"

"I know." He motioned for me to go on toward the village itself.

The silence here felt heavy as a grave, broken only by the groaning of the wind through the tree branches. It wasn't that late at night, was it? Maybe nine?

The wind rushed through the trees, making the boughs creak above us. Among the oaks and rowans, I squeezed out my wet hair, then started walking toward the forest's edge. Except there were no lights like there should have been. The village should have been lit up at this time of night, but we had only the moonlight lighting our way.

Here, the trees' boughs seemed to arch protectively above us. I glanced at a gnarled oak—just by the spot where I'd hidden the day Ruadan had invaded.

I reached for Ruadan's hand, taking comfort in its warmth. The breeze toyed with his pale hair. An ancient fae prince like him belonged in the forest. Just not this forest. The image in my mind of his invasion felt so vivid here. He'd been *terrifying.* A god of war.

At the forest's edge, my heart was racing out of control. Dark buildings all around, not a sign of life anywhere. "There should be lights," I whispered.

I swallowed hard. Through the trees, I had a view of Eden. Timber-frame houses crowded narrow roads, just as they always had. A temple to the Old Gods stood in the center of the village, and I could see its elegant stone roof from here, the tallest building in Eden. Everything was just as it should be.

Except life was completely absent from this place. I

couldn't even sense a blackbird's heartbeat. Chilly wind whipped over my skin and hair.

As we stepped into the clearing, a heavy weight pressed on my chest, and I stared at the darkness before me. I released Ruadan's hand and broke into a run for the nearest building, just on the village's edge.

A thin layer of dust coated wooden shutters. I unhooked the shutters, then pulled them open. They creaked apart to reveal dark windows. I cupped my hands to peer inside the glass. This had been the bakery once, but now dust and cobwebs coated the furniture. My throat went dry.

"There's no one here," I said to Ruadan.

"But Adonis will be here. Even Adonis couldn't get out of a locked world."

He had a point. But what sort of state would I find him in?

I turned to survey the dirt road that wound into the center of Eden, where the temple stood. Just like in the shadow void, the buildings were dark and shuttered.

Ruadan's fingers twitched at his hilt, and he sniffed the air. "Something isn't right here."

I swallowed hard. "Yeah. Well, I mean, I did kill everyone, so that is probably the thing that feels a bit wrong."

He shook his head. "No. I feel magic here. I just don't know where it's coming from."

"What kind of magic?"

His brow furrowed. "Fae magic, I think."

Hope lit in my chest. Fae magic. My mother had powerful fae magic. Was she still around somewhere?

Quietly, we followed the path deeper into the village, and I gripped Ruadan's hand hard. The dirt path wound around the buildings, toward the village green. The temple stood on a gently rolling hill.

And before the temple, I found piles of rocks—silvery

light streamed over dozens of them, in little crooked pyramids. Dried floral wreaths rested on top of the piles. The sight of them was a punch to my gut. These were fae grave markers.

One of the wreaths caught my eye—dried honeysuckle and crimson anemones. My parents' favorite flowers, intertwined. My legs felt weak, and I gripped Ruadan's arm to steady myself.

Where was my dad? Someone had buried the dead, which meant he couldn't be among them. Not to mention the fact that my powers wouldn't kill him.

"Where would we be most likely to find him?" asked Ruadan, trying to keep me focused.

The tremors in my hands had returned. "We should look in my old house."

I let go of Ruadan again, and I broke into a run, feet pounding on the dirt road. My parents' home wasn't far from the green, near the burbling brook. I was nearly there—nearly to my dad.

I turned off the path, running in the tall grasses outside my old home, where wildflowers dappled the ground.

It was too dark. Just like the others, it looked like an empty vessel. I ground to a halt, investigating it. Vines covered the house's exterior like nature was trying to suffocate it, and moonflowers blossomed all over them. Where the hells could my father have gone if he wasn't here?

Our house didn't have shutters, and I cupped my hands to peer through the dusty glass window. I couldn't see much beyond the grime—but the Angel of Death did not live in grime. Clearly, Adonis was not here. Still, maybe I could find a clue of some kind that would tell me what had happened to him.

"I'm going in," I said.

I shivered as I pushed through the door into the darkened

cottage. Behind me, Ruadan chanted in Ancient Fae, and he called up a sphere of golden light that cast a warm glow over my house.

The orb floated into the old living room, casting a dull amber glow over the dust. I coughed, my gaze sweeping over the table where we'd eaten dinner, and the chaise lounge where I'd sat in my mum's lap for stories.

With a lump in my throat, I crossed to the ornately carved mantle. Among the carvings of leaves and flowers, I was searching for the moon and the word "Bug."

But when I drew closer, my heart constricted. The moon carving was there—but my nickname wasn't. No "Bug." I frowned at it, tracing over it with my fingertips. Everything was just as it had been, except that one little detail.

The shock of it disoriented me, and it felt like I'd been erased from history. Now, the ground no longer felt quite so solid beneath my feet. Had I somehow imagined that detail of my life?

Dizzy, I felt as if my spirit were curling into the air like fog. I wasn't sure what was real anymore. The fae, the gladiator, the death angel—all the different Lioras vying for control, none of them stable, none rooted to the earth. Which one was real? I closed my eyes, overcome by the feeling that I was watching myself from the outside. Here was a woman who'd probably lost her mind long ago.

For one wild, dizzying moment, I had the horrifying thought that I'd never left Baleros's cage—that this was all something I'd dreamt up to make myself into a hero. It was the escape route of a broken spirit.

My breath heaved in my chest. No, it had ended even earlier than that. Maybe I'd died that day, when Ruadan had come, that day I'd killed everyone else—

"Liora?"

Ruadan's deep voice called me back to reality.

His violet eyes surveyed me with concern. He must have read the sheer terror and confusion in my eyes, because he touched the side of my face, painfully gently. His magic snaked down my body—a firm touch that warmed me and seemed to fuse itself to the floor, steadying me. Tendrils of his magic wrapped around my ankles and feet.

I'm here.

"Thanks."

His magic had grounded me, and somehow he'd known to do it instinctively.

With his magic helping to stabilize me, I looked up at him —at those violet eyes that were sometimes so cold. "I don't understand what's happening," I said. "My dad engraved my nickname into that mantle a long time ago. I remember it really clearly. It should say 'Bug.'"

"While you were inspecting that, I was trying to get a read on the magic here. There is magic all around us."

I frowned at the mantle, then cocked my head. "Are you sure you took us to the right place?" I asked. "What if it's a replica?"

He shot me a disbelieving look. "Of course I took us to the right place."

I ran my fingertips over that moon carving. "Is it possible this place is glamoured? That the real world is hidden some-where under this one?"

"It's possible. But it would take someone extremely skilled at fae glamour to pull it off."

"That's why I asked. My mother was brilliant with glam-our. Unfortunately, I didn't inherit her skills." I bit my lip. "Shit. Whatever is happening, Adonis isn't here. And I promised the Shadow Fae I'd be fast. We may not have a ton of time until they succumb to the Plague."

"I think you could heal them."

I shook my head, still staring at the mantle. I frowned at

it. I hadn't noticed it at first, but on the lower ridge of the mantle, a line cut through the wood—nearly imperceptible at first among the intricate carvings of leaves and berries.

I gripped the top and bottom of the mantle, jaw dropping as I slid a section away to reveal a hollow alcove. "This is new."

Inside the alcove lay a small, folded piece of paper. As Ruadan looked on, I unfolded it, my heart stuttering.

Find Aenor.

Was it my mother's cursive handwriting? I think it was. And that meant she was alive.

"What does it say?" asked Ruadan.

"Find Aenor." I met his gaze. "Any idea who or what Aenor is?"

He pulled the paper from my hands, frowning at it. "Aenor. Flayer of Skins, Scourge of the Wicked."

"She sounds … nice. They want me to find her? Any idea why? Or where she might be?"

"We can find out."

"How do you know her name?"

"She's on our kill list, but she wasn't a priority."

"Of course. She has useful magical powers, which means you want to kill her."

"We don't know that they're useful."

"If my parents are sending us to her, she has useful powers. My parents knew that I'd check the mantle to see my name. They didn't want anyone else to find this, but they wanted me to see it."

"You sound certain that your mother is alive."

I smiled, a weight lifting off me. "I think it's her handwriting. I think my father brought her back."

"Let's search the rest of the house and the rest of Eden as fast as we can. If we sniff for your father's scent and shadow-leap, we can cover a lot of ground fast."

I nodded, though I already felt in my bones they weren't here. I shadow-leapt through the house, finding it nearly exactly as I'd left it. Then, we whooshed through the abandoned town, through the homes and the cemetery on the green, through the woods and the temple. And as we searched, I clutched that piece of paper in my hand. Wind rushed over me as we moved swiftly around Eden.

This was turning into a much more complicated recovery mission than I'd hoped.

Once we'd sniffed out every building and scoured the forest, we were certain that Adonis wasn't here. And I was sure this wasn't the real Eden anymore.

Near the cemetery green, Ruadan opened another portal. We were returning to the Institute empty-handed, and nothing had changed yet.

But now, I had a tiny shred of evidence my mother could be alive.

CHAPTER 14

*S*odden with portal water, we crawled onto the Institute's Tower Green. A canopy of night still arched above us; the moon shone bright with Nyxobas's power.

As I stood, the air began to chill around us, the moon burning brighter in the sky. I turned to look at Ruadan.

Except he was no longer Ruadan. Now, Nyxobas's crescent of silver horns beamed from his skull. His body had grown, and night magic billowed around him like smoke from a bellows.

I pushed my damp hair out of my eyes. "Hey, Nyxobas. Any chance you can turn up the temperature on your portal water? The knights are dying."

No response—just those eerie, silver eyes. A whorl of shadows consumed Ruadan.

Beneath my feet, the earth rumbled. What the hells was happening now? We had to find Aenor. I desperately wanted to get to my parents as soon as I could, but Nyxobas was interfering.

"You're a god," I grumbled. "You could just tell us who the traitor is."

In the center of the courtyard, the grassy earth cracked open, and I held out my arms to balance myself as the void gaped open before us. I backed away from it, not eager for another trip into a hell world.

When I looked up again, Nyxobas had shifted. He now stood at the edge of the portal, holding Niall by the neck. In his other hand, he gripped a Shadow Fae named Turi. Both of them had pale lips, and they were barely able to keep their eyes open. They looked at me expectantly, hoping I'd brought back a cure for them. I just shook my head with a pang of guilt.

The chokehold Nyxobas had on them probably wasn't helping the situation. He really was an arsehole. These knights were his servants. They had dedicated their souls to him, and he treated them like this.

Nyxobas threw both of them into the portal, and they sank deep into the darkness. The surface smoothed over once more, turning to ice.

Nyxobas turned to me, his glacial gaze boring into me.

I didn't want to be with the remote god of the void right now. I wanted Ruadan back, and I wanted to find my parents. I was still clutching the tiny piece of paper that had held Acnor's name, but the portal water had washed my mother's handwriting away.

I vaguely registered the other knights arriving as I stared down at the ruined paper.

A touch on my arm called my attention away from it, and I looked up at Melusine's sickly face. Her lips were parched, and dark circles hung beneath her eyes. She smelled faintly of vomit.

"Where's your dad?" she asked.

I shook my head. "I'm sorry. We didn't find him. We have

a lead, though. Someone named Aenor, Flayer of Skins. Does that ring any bells?"

Her expression looked dejected, and she held up her hands, addressing the rest of them. "No death angel. I see no death angel, no father, and I put two and two together. We're screwed. We're all gonna die—"

"Shhh…" I cut in. "That's not good for morale. I'm working on it."

She pulled her cloak around herself more tightly. "Who's in the void?"

"Turi and Niall."

"I need to lie down and get some rest before he throws me in."

As she stumbled away, Nyxobas stalked toward me. I eyed him with surprise. Why was he studying me so closely? Even if he was in my lover's body, he unnerved me completely. I gave him my best *back off* glare.

The look did absolutely nothing to put him off, which I suppose made sense, since he was a night god who'd fallen from the heavens and lived tens of thousands of years in Hell. My narrowed eyes were not going to strike fear into his heart.

When he was just a foot away, he stared down at me. "Life and death mingle within you," he said, his voice the oddly dissonant sound of young and old people speaking at once. "The beginning and the end. Seeds growing from the ashes."

What do you say to that? "Okay. Thanks." This wasn't helpful information. But maybe he *could* help with something. "Do you know anyone called the Flayer of Skins, by any chance?"

His attention darted back to the portal, where the ice began to crack.

Of course he didn't provide any useful information. The gods never did.

A fist hammered at the ice—then another. Both Niall and Turi were fighting their way out. I would stay just long enough to see their heads breach the surface.

My fists tightened. "Is there a less grueling way you would test the knights? They're very sick."

His attention remained on the cracking portal. "It refreshes me to feel your spirits in the void."

"But they're dying. They're your servants."

"Fix it, then." His voice seemed to come from a million miles away.

Simple as that. Just—fix it. "How?"

He whirled, then he cupped my face with his icy hand. Emptiness spun through my body as I stared into his glacial, silvery eyes and took in his stark beauty.

He leaned in and whispered, "You know how this ends, don't you?"

"It ends with us imprisoning Baleros."

His breath was a frigid breeze on the shell of my ear. "It ends with Ruadan's death."

The words crashed into me like a wave. Ruadan had said that Nyxobas didn't lie. He knew the future, and he spoke the truth.

"If you know so much, why don't you help us?" My fingers tightened into fists. "It's not going to happen. I won't let it." My promise felt like a lie. What control did I have over any of this? "He's your grandson," I added, although I knew he didn't care.

Shadows writhed around him, obscuring his face.

I backed away from him, surveying the other Shadow Fae again. Barry looked like he was going to be sick. He held a hand over his mouth, hunching over while the two knights fought to break out of the ice.

At last, a booming crack filled the air, and a large fissure split the ice.

I tried not to think about Nyxobas's prediction, but I felt like the world had been pulled out from under my feet.

At last, a hand slammed through the ice, piercing it completely. Within moments, Turi was hauling himself out, and he rolled onto the grass. On his hands and knees, he vomited up blood, and I winced. Niall was out a moment later, heaving for breath, his body convulsing as he scrambled to find purchase on the ice.

I rushed over to him and grabbed his arms, pulling him out of the shattered ice. As soon as his legs were clear, the ice melted away, steam rising into the air.

Nyxobas was already scanning the knights for his next victim.

I wasn't doing much good here, watching this. And if Ruadan wasn't available to help me learn about Aenor, I'd have to try to discover this information on my own.

Behind me, another knight whimpered as Nyxobas gripped him by the throat, ready to slam him into the cold.

Where else could I find out about Aenor? If my parents knew her, perhaps she'd been in Eden, too. Or maybe she'd visited before the worlds had closed for good.

I started pacing, the cogs in my mind turning.

There was only one other person in the Institute who'd lived in Eden. And while he might be mad, Demented Mike could have some answers buried in his addled brain. He'd been there when our world ended, and he'd been there before.

I shadow-leapt over to Melusine, who lay on the grass, and I gently tapped her shoulder to wake her. She blinked, her dark eyes taking a moment to focus.

"Melusine?" I asked softly. "Do you know anything about a potion or tonic that could help clear someone's addled mind?"

"Of course I know something like that." She started to stand.

I stopped her with a gentle hand. "Just tell me how to make it, then go back to sleep."

"In the herbarium, you'll find mandrake, dragon's blood, a gryphon's saliva, and Earl Grey tea."

I blinked. "Earl Grey?"

"I know, it's disgusting, but it's a necessary part of the spell. Boil it all together into a tonic, and it will clear the patient's head." Her eyes were heavy-lidded, and they started to close again.

"Wait, Melusine?"

"Yes?"

"If Nyxobas leaves Ruadan's body any time soon, tell him I went to find Demented Mike."

"Sure thing."

A smile curled my lips. If this tonic worked, it would bring about my first meaningful conversation with someone from Eden in over ten years.

$\mathcal{I}$ clutched the warm brew and hurried down the hall toward Demented Mike's room. In Eden, he'd been one of my best friends. Two years older than me, but tolerant of me following him around. He'd wanted to be human, for some bizarre reason, and he used to teach me all the dirty words he knew.

In the hallway, moonlight streamed through the peaked windows onto the floor, and I glanced for a moment at the trials going on outside. With any luck, they'd all be over soon.

I pushed open the door to his room, and light beamed in from the hallway. He lay flat on his stomach in the dark, his palms pressed against the flagstones. His cheeks had the pinkish hue of fever, and sweat beaded on his face.

Shit. The plague magic was still pulsing around the Institute, infecting people. And Mike had caught it.

He turned to look at me, his eyes wide, and he snarled. "I Gmm, the Noe I Ainml I called Nma please…" he hissed from the floor.

He was speaking fragments of a demon tongue he

must've picked up in the shadow void. I had no idea what he was saying.

"So, I brought you some hot tea." I left the steaming mug on the floor, and he scuttled over to it on his hands and knees. "I think it might help things a bit."

He lapped tea from the cup like a cat. Then, he looked up at me, his eyes wide. "Here I kad Amman roots ktzsnc embers shhhh krditzsmtz I demon mrrnkg aisa hee cnhnma miracle."

I sat on the edge of his bed, and light from the moon beamed into the dark room. "Okay, so, I would love to reconnect with you, Mike, but I think we have a little work to do to get you back to your old form."

He slurped the tea. "Darkness...."

"I know. It was bad in the void. I'm sorry." I closed my eyes, trying not to think of what might've happened to the others I'd killed. I had to keep it together right now, long enough to save the Institute. "Mike, does the name Aenor ring a bell?"

He sat up now, and he stared at me. He took another long sip of his tea, his clouded expression clearing a little. I waited with him in silence while he slurped it.

"I have some questions to ask you, when you're ready."

"I ... a darkness." He cocked his head, looking suddenly more alert. "There were no other fae in the void. Just me. I heard people speaking to me, even though you weren't there. I heard you speaking to me sometimes. The gods are hungry for souls, and they care for nothing else. They think the souls of others will fill the emptiness ... but it never does. One god, split into seven, tormented ever since. In the hell worlds, we feel the pain of the gods."

He stared at the floor, lost in his thoughts.

"I met some other demons after a while." Another sip of

tea. "They kept me company. I learned bits of their languages. Then, after an eternity passed, I saw you."

"I'm sorry." Guilt twisted inside me. How did I explain this to him? "Thing is, it turns out I'm a death angel, and I didn't know. And when the fae army invaded, um … a whole bunch of death magic exploded from me and killed everyone by accident. I'm not yet sure what happened to the others, and I'm just trying to put together the pieces and find my dad to help me."

He drank another sip. "I know what happened. The voices told me in the void. It's okay. You weren't in control of it. I understand. The gods are in control. They're always in control. And the gods will have their souls."

We were getting somewhere. Coming to Demented Mike was the best idea I'd had in a while.

"Do you know what happened to everyone else?" I asked.

He nodded. "Of course. Your father brought them back from the dead."

My heart leapt. The first good news I'd had in ages. "My mum, too?"

"Everyone but me. He could never find me. I fell in too deep. I started turning demon fast, machalail grumm slut puppet." He closed his eyes, taking another sip of the tea. "Only you could find me. Your powers are like his, but maybe stronger. Both of you can lift this illness I have. This death magic. And as long as you both live, you can raise each other from the grave."

Alive. Despite everything happening, I beamed with joy. "Okay. This is good. This is helpful. Do you know why Eden is empty? We opened the portal and we found only graves."

He shook his head.

"Do you know where my father is?" I pressed, desperate now.

"Eden."

"I couldn't find him there."

Hope bubbled in my chest anyway. My mum was alive. Everyone I'd killed in Eden was alive again. I'd find my family again. I was certain we could get my dad to help us cure the Shadow Fae—and to imprison Baleros forever.

"Mike, have you ever heard the name Aenor?" I asked. "When I went into Eden, I couldn't find my parents. But I did find a note from them that said to find Aenor. I think she must be someone who can help me. Then I can get you back to your family."

He traced the rim of his teacup with his fingertip. "Aenor. Aenor. Aenor," he muttered. "Flayer of Skins, Scourge of the Wicked."

"Yes! That's her. How do you know her?"

"She visited your father sometimes. Before the worlds closed for good."

"Where would I find her?"

He frowned. "I don't remember what she looked like. Just that she smelled of honey and soil. And lemony flowers, and mossy limestone. And she gave me a human finger bone. She sells them, I think."

Aenor, Flayer of Skins, who reeked of honey and dirt and sold human bones. She sounded lovely.

"I'm tired. Noe I Ainml." Mike closed his eyes once more and curled up on the floor, muttering to himself in Demonic. His teeth chattered.

I pulled the soft wool blanket off the bed and covered his shivering body with it. I crossed to his window. From here, I had a view of the Tower Green, and Nyxobas was gripping another knight by the throat. I couldn't even see who it was. Melusine, maybe? He hurled them into the void and another brutal trial began.

I turned to rush outside. I had a few more facts to go on now, but I needed help interpreting what they meant.

CHAPTER 16

I crossed out onto the Tower Green once more, and the sound of shrieking pierced the night calm. Nyxobas stood before Barry, whose face had gone completely white, his body rigid. Barry opened and closed his mouth a few times as if he were trying to speak. His lumen stone glowed faintly under his shirt.

"Do you have something to say?" Nyxobas's voice sent a chill snaking up my spine.

"Had no control," Barry stammered. "You know. You know. You *know.* I had no control. Baleros controls me."

Nyxobas grabbed him by the throat, and Barry started to choke. He was still trying to speak, and he was able to get out the words "necklace" and "control."

I caught my breath. That necklace around his throat—the one I'd seen in the dungeon—had Baleros given it to him?

Before Barry could utter another word, Nyxobas hurled him into the portal.

Barry's body sank beneath the watery surface, and the necklace along with him. Cold magic rushed over my body like an icy wind. Then, I stared as the earth began to close again, the ground trembling. Grass and soil shifted and sealed over the portal.

So. That was our traitor.

An interrogation would have been useful, but that was not how Nyxobas operated.

When the portal had sealed over completely, I glanced at Nyxobas—still the pale, gleaming eyes of the god and tattoos that shifted over his forearms.

His pale eyes were locked on me, and my chest hollowed out. Then, the violet in Ruadan's eyes returned, and I let out a breath as the real Grand Master returned. The other knights were sitting around the sealed portal, shaking in their cloaks.

Melusine clutched a hot cup of tea, her hair drenched. "Good. That's over. Barry was the traitor, and we can all move on with our lives."

"Our very short lives," said Aengus through chattering teeth, "considering we are about a day away from death. Where is the Horseman?"

I shook my head. "I don't know yet. I'm still working—"

"Then you have to try to help us!" shouted Aengus. "At least try."

"And if I make it worse?" I asked.

"Don't make it worse," said Aengus.

Ruadan's body had gone completely still, and his violet eyes burned in the gloom. "I know that you have the power within you, but you might not be ready just yet. It's your choice, Liora. We can still try to find Adonis."

I rubbed a knot in my forehead. "I'll try. I just think I'll need alcohol." Then, I stared at the grass in the courtyard. Something wasn't sitting right with me. Something besides my upcoming task. "But, I'm not quite ready to move on from the Barry situation yet. I mean, don't you think Baleros could have sent someone more competent than Barry?"

"He was talking about his necklace," Melusine added from over her tea. "Something about control. Like it wasn't his fault."

I glanced at Ruadan. "So you didn't give him that lumen stone? I saw it on him in prison. Just for a moment."

Ruadan shook his head. "That necklace didn't come from us. Charmed, probably, with powers of mind control. Barry was a pawn."

"The necklace was beaming with shadow magic." I ran my fingers through my hair. "I just don't feel like this is the whole answer. Maddan said the traitor was someone I knew. He said that Baleros had a powerful ally. Barry was neither of those things."

The night wind toyed with Ruadan's hair. "I'm sure that wasn't the entirety of Baleros's plans. Everyone will remain on high alert until we've locked Baleros in our dungeons forever, chained with iron."

I breathed in deeply. "When Nyxobas is in your body, do you remember what he says?"

"Most of it." Then he frowned, his body still. "But he said something to you, and it's a blank. I can't remember it at all. What was it?"

When I thought of Nyxobas's prophecy, I just wanted to wrap my arms around Ruadan and keep him close. I wanted him in that hot bath with me forever, locked away safely in his room. And most of all, like a lioness, my instinct was to destroy anyone who would come near him. I longed to tear their flesh off their bones, to turn their bodies to dust. I even wanted to destroy Nyxobas for what he'd said.

My love for Ruadan was a raging fire.

Darkness coiled around him. "What did he say to you?" he pressed.

It didn't matter, because I wasn't going to let him die, no matter what the prophecy said. "He just said that we faced danger. Nothing we don't already know." After Ruadan's insistence that I trust him, the lie tasted like poison in my mouth.

But the thing was, Ruadan had a tendency to try to sacrifice himself—just like he had at Hampton Court Palace, when he'd tried to give himself over to Baleros. If Ruadan thought this was the ending—that he was destined to die—he might rush into it. I saw no reason to hasten that option.

"Look." I gestured at the knights, who were sitting on the grass, most of them shivering and sweating at the same time. "Let's get them all inside to the hall. I'll have a bit of whiskey to calm my death instinct, and I'll see what I can do."

"Now, please," said Aengus. "We don't have time for you to fruitlessly search the world for your father. My fingers are about to rot off. I think the tips of my toes have started to go necrotic."

I glanced around at the Shadow Fae, all of them silent, staring at me. A painful-looking lump had formed on Aengus's neck, and a red rash had climbed over Niall's face.

Already, I could feel the wings at my shoulder blades aching to come out.

So I was supposed to cure them, but I had no idea how. Right now, I felt about as competent as a dog sitting at a desk with a pencil to complete his income tax returns.

Would instinct take over and show me the way, or would I simply kill everyone in the city?

I guess we were about to find out.

* * *

IN THE GREAT HALL, the knights sat at tables over steaming cups of tea, looking at me expectantly. I'd had enough whiskey to give me a good buzz, and I now felt much more confident about the situation. I was a death angel, and I could do this.

Ruadan touched my arm. "Are you sure you're ready to try?"

"I think so. I'm feeling better about it. And Demented Mike said I was as powerful as my dad."

"Demented Mike?"

I bit my lip. "Granted, his nickname probably doesn't inspire much confidence in his pronouncements. Anyway, he's the demon-fae I pulled from the shadow void. He thinks I can do it."

Ruadan nodded, then stepped away from me. I closed my eyes, trying to summon my angel side. Someone's coughs echoed off the high, stone ceiling. I waited for my wings to burst out of me.

Nothing was happening, and I could practically feel the frustration of everyone around me. How did I make this happen?

Someone—Aengus, probably—let out a dramatic, exasperated sigh.

I opened one of my eyes to see what was happening. Just the knights, glaring at me from their wool blankets, steam from tea curling around them.

"Just give me a minute," I muttered.

The last times I'd transformed, I'd been panicking: when Ruadan had invaded Eden, when I'd thought he was going to die at Hampton Court Palace, when I thought he might be dying within the Tower. So, I just had to channel that sense of panic, that primal flame of protectiveness.

I glanced at Ruadan and the World Key glowing at his neck. Nyxobas said this ended with Ruadan's death. Baleros planned to slaughter my lover, to cut the skin off his body. Wild, protective fury roiled in my chest as I looked at him. I wanted to rip Baleros limb from limb, to spread his bones and flesh to the far corners of the earth so I could keep my love safe.

That flame in my heart ignited, and electric power shot down my shoulder blades. My shoulders flung back, arms stiffening.

I'll bury your bodies in long-forgotten graves. The yews will feed from your flesh.

Euphoria ripped through me, and wings erupted from my back, lifting me higher, toward the rib-vaulted ceiling. Why did death feel so glorious?

Now, I simply needed to control the death magic, to pull it away from the Shadow Fae. Except, I didn't really feel in control. In fact—

The Great Hall below me seemed to fall away, and I was no longer in the Institute, but back in my cage, covered in dirt. Ciara snored by my side, and Baleros stood above me, grinning down at me. "Let's let the little monster out of her cage, shall we?"

The gate creaked open, setting me free to do the one thing I was good at. The one thing the monster had been born for.

Killing.

When I'd crossed into the ring that day, sword at my waist, I'd been expecting the usual opponents: a cyclops, a demon, a horde of vampires. Instead, I found a scrawny teenage boy. With his peach fuzz mustache, acne, and terrified expression, he looked oddly human.

But Baleros had trained me well. I knew never to underestimate my opponent, no matter how weak he looked. I knew that survival meant striking first. *Baleros's seventh law of power: Kill or be killed.* Hesitation meant death. The scrawny boy before me was likely a shapeshifter, disguising himself as an innocent.

It wasn't until my blade went through his neck, when I

saw the blood and the bone and the piss staining his jeans, that I'd understood the real situation. He was just as he'd appeared—a terrified human boy.

As the crowd stared at me in stunned silence, their expressions told me everything I needed to know. This had been a different sort of lesson from Baleros. The lesson here was not one of survival.

The lesson was that I was a monster.

And monsters belonged in cages, didn't they?

Someone was calling my name now—screaming it, in fact.

The image of the arena thinned, until I found myself in the Great Hall once more, hovering above the knights. Now, the only sound was my wings beating the air.

"Liora!" It was Ruadan. "Stop."

I looked down at the Shadow Fae, my gaze roaming over Melusine, Aengus, Turi.... To my horror, they looked *worse*. Melusine's skin had taken on a greenish hue, and her eyes had closed. The glands in her neck were purplish with swelling. Aengus lay sleeping, his chest still rising and falling.

Only Ruadan was still standing.

My wings retracted, shooting back into my body. I fell *hard* to the stone floor.

This had been a terrible idea. I was made only to kill, not to heal. They never should have counted on me.

I pushed myself up to my feet, dusting off my body. My failure was crushing, and I felt it like a pain in my chest. "I'm sorry. I don't know how to control this power."

"You haven't had time to learn," said Ruadan.

If Baleros didn't live in my mind, would it have worked?

Melusine groaned, her eyelids heavy. "Fix this."

I gripped my purple hair, ready to pull it out. "I will. I will. I just need to get to my dad."

Ruadan touched my shoulder. "We'll find Aenor. We will

get to your father. We can search the Tower's records for references to her whereabouts."

"Searching records sounds slightly time-consuming. Okay, tell me if this means anything to you. Any idea where we would find someone who sold human finger bones and smelled of soil, honey, lemony flowers, and limestone?"

"Black elder tree. They have lemon-scented flowers."

"You are full of amazing facts."

He scrubbed a hand over his mouth. "Black elder trees and limestones—the London Wall, by Barbican. She's underground, perhaps, because of the soil and the fact that you're generally not allowed to sell bones above ground."

I gripped him by the shoulders. "Good. Good. We have a location. I'm getting my lumen stone and my bug-out bag, and we're going to find this bone-selling freak."

And it *had* to work, because the Shadow Fae wouldn't survive much longer.

CHAPTER 17

I gripped my bug-out bag, trying to push out thoughts of my failure and of the knights dying in the Great Hall. I still had a bit of a buzz from the whiskey, but it wasn't enough to lift my dark mood.

This time, we'd come armed. I had no idea what we were going to find when we met Aenor, Flayer of Skins, but everything I'd learned about her so far led me to believe she was a complete psycho. And if I *really* needed to, I could always beckon the mist army to me.

We'd shadow-leapt to Barbican in only a few minutes. Here, moonlight and the distant glow of streetlights illuminated the crumbling old Roman wall. Empty windows in the wall gaped like dark wounds. Once, it had protected the city from barbarians. Now, it was just an ancient fragment, a testament to a forgotten London that intersected with a serene canal.

We were sniffing the air, trying to home in on the scent of lemony blossoms and human bones. The damp breeze skimmed my skin. I had the sense that in this ancient part of

London, we were walking over layers of lives, centuries of souls that now still clung to the crumbling rock wall.

Ruadan inhaled deeply. "Honey," he said. "That's the one scent not native to this place. It must belong to Aenor. We're in the right place."

At last, we were getting somewhere, and my pulse raced with anticipation. I sniffed the air too, and after a moment, I got a faint whiff of honey.

To our right, modern apartments loomed over a placid canal, but Ruadan had thought Aenor might be underground. Now, I tuned into a powerful magic that thrummed through the air. It felt like the music of string instruments vibrating over my skin. Was that Aenor?

Ruadan pointed at a squat tower inset into the Roman wall. "The scent of honey is coming from there."

He led me around the corner to a dark alcove within the wall —a hollowed-out tower, one side of it collapsed. The dark canal flowed serenely by its side. I couldn't see much in the darkness —just grass and the crumbling tower, overgrown with plants.

"Honey and lemony blossoms," I whispered.

Ruadan caught my eye. "When we meet her, be cautious. We don't really know what the note meant."

I frowned. "I suppose." A terrible thought twisted in my skull. "You don't think this could be a trick played by Baleros, do you?"

Ruadan shook his head. "Baleros had no way to get into Eden. But we should be careful anyway. Things could have changed since your mother wrote that note. Just don't announce who you are right away, until we learn more about her."

"Okay, fair enough."

Ruadan crouched down. "She's here." He reared back his arm, then rammed his fist into the earth, all the way up to his elbow. He moved his arm around for a moment, seemingly grasping something.

Then, with a groaning sound, he pulled up a wooden hatch door. And as he did, the faint smell of honey and lemon hit me—along with the metallic scent of blood.

Aenor.

But before we could leap in, the sound of hissing echoed off the stone behind us. My pulse racing, I whirled.

A small horde of vampires was moving for us. There were at least twelve of them—large, ancient vampires, their movements swift and precise, fangs bared, armed with swords. Odd. Vampires usually just used their teeth and hands.

My blade was already out, and Ruadan drew his sword, ready to take them on.

A dark smile curled my lips. It had been far too long since I'd killed anything, and bloodlust pounded through my veins. The angel of death in me was stirring once more. Gods, there were a lot of them. They must've been lying in wait.

I will slake my thirst on your blood.

I let my body fill with the ancient shadow magic of the lumen stone, and I leapt closer to the vampires, touching down on the stones with a swing of my sword. My blade hacked through the first vampire's neck, slicing off his head. The winds of battle rushed through me, and I pivoted, attacking another vamp.

My sword clashed with his, sparking in the night. Soon, I was moving like a storm wind, whirling and ducking as we fought.

Ruadan fought by my side, gracefully attacking. Clouds of ash darkened the air around us as we killed the vampires. My wings ached to emerge, but I fought hard to keep them down. The last appearance of my angelic side had not gone well.

Pivot, strike, carve.... I drove my sword through the heart of a female vampire, then through her neck. Her body dissolved into ash so thick I coughed.

My blood thundered as more vamps crawled from the shadows. Why did they keep coming for us, when they saw death awaited them? Maybe we were outnumbered, but they were on suicide missions.

I rip open your veins. I cover your eyes, fill your mouth with soil.

The tip of a blade swiped me from behind, but I danced away from it, nearly losing my balance.

The vamps were all around us—too many for this to be a coincidence. It was at this point that I noticed the gleaming magical necklaces around their throats.

Baleros was controlling them, just like he'd controlled Barry. They were mindlessly following his orders.

Pivot, strike, carve.

Ash rained around us as the vampires met their final deaths. I stole a quick glance at Ruadan. His savage grace, brutal and controlled, took my breath away.

Pivot, strike, carve.

I inhaled clouds of cinders. Where the hells were they all coming from?

Somehow, Baleros had been watching us closely.

Death kissed my skin as I moved among them, ushering them to their final graves.

I will end you all.

From shadows all over the courtyard, crawling from behind the Roman wall, through its gaping windows—more and more vamps were coming for us. Now, a sharp coil of panic curled around my heart.

Each one of them wore a glowing, magic necklace—and they all wanted to slaughter Ruadan. Baleros had been watching us, either through spies or a scrying mirror, and he'd sent his entire army here to slaughter us.

I took a step back toward the Roman wall, quickly getting backed into a corner. My pulse was racing out of control, but I didn't want to unleash the monster now.

We needed help.

As I swung my sword in increasingly wild arcs, I whispered the spell for the mist soldiers. *"Mogidellior deusaman."*

As soon as the spell was out of my mouth, a thick fog curled around the vampiric mob, until I could hardly see them.

I leapt up to one of the crumbling tower walls, crouching on a stony outcrop. From there, I used the few fae commands I knew to control the mist soldiers. I changed the shapes of the soldiers, transforming them into beasts that ripped the vampires apart.

"Aerouant dispennior."

A group of mist soldiers melded together into a dragon with enormous teeth, and the creature roared. It slashed at the vampires with its talons, its ethereal body tinged with moonlight.

"Diaoull lazannior."

Beastly creatures formed from the mist with talons the length of swords, teeth sharp as iron spikes, tails like thorny maces that crushed the vampires' limbs.

"Evell dispennior."

Birds as large as pterodactyls formed from fog swooped down, plucking up the vampires, carrying them away.

My monstrous mist soldiers picked off one vampire after another, tearing them to shreds, dragging them away until we had only a small crowd left. Then, I leapt back down into the fray—not far from Ruadan. He was still fighting viciously, unfatigued, and I started fighting alongside him.

I drove my blade through the heart of another vamp. His body started to slump, and I gripped his hand. A tattoo marked his skin—the bundle of sticks. Baleros's symbol. No surprises there.

I let him fall to the ground, then I severed his head. With only a few vampires remaining, it was time to get some information before they were all dead.

"Ruadan!" I shouted, fending off another attacker. "Cover me. I need to torture someone."

A statuesque, brunette vamp lunged for me, her sword raised. I gripped the hilt of my own sword, blood pumping hard. Behind me, I could hear Ruadan's blade clashing with our attackers. I had no doubt he could hold his own with these numbers.

I felt as if sharpened claws were stroking down my shoulder blades, making me shiver. My wings ached to emerge, but I kept in control.

"I am the beginning and the end." I spoke the words quietly, but they echoed off the stone around us. *I am your broken spirit as pain eats your body. I am the insects that make their home in your flesh.*

The vamp looked startled, her eyes widening as her attacks grew slower. I was holding back, unwilling to unleash my death magic—and yet the force of my presence struck fear into her. Fog coiled around her in thick tendrils.

Good. I seemed to terrify her so much I didn't actually need to torture her.

I took a step closer. She started shaking, frozen in place.

My fingers twitched. "Stay here and tell me what I want to know, vampire, and I'll let you live."

I gripped her by the throat, lifting her into the air. I could read the terror on her features—the silent, abject horror of her final death.

My wings were desperate to emerge, but I couldn't lose control completely again. "Do you understand what I'm saying, vampire?"

She nodded mutely.

"Do you work for Baleros?" I asked.

She nodded again.

"Where is he?"

"A … a church. I think. We're not supposed to know which one." She was struggling to speak—possibly because I was nearly crushing her throat, but I didn't want to let her go.

"Which church?"

"I don't know the name." Her body trembled. "But I can tell you something else! He gave something to the god of night. A ring. Some kind of magic ring. A cage. It had—"

Her eyes bulged wide, and a gagging sound rose from her throat. Then, her eyes went dull and dead.

Had I broken her?

But when I looked down at the vampire, I saw that it wasn't me who'd killed her. No, the tip of a long, iron knife protruded from her chest. Before my eyes, her body crumbled into a pile of dust, the iron knife clanging beside it.

What the hells?

I looked up, and my heart skipped a beat. There—another angel in the sky, his wings thumping the air like a war drum. The moon haloed his head, making it hard to see his face.

My breath left my lungs. Dad?

He was holding another knife—one aimed right at me. My chest constricted, and time seemed to slow down, the night wind rushing over me. Why did he look like he wanted to kill me?

When he threw the knife, I dodged. It narrowly missed my chest.

I breathed out. Not Adonis, then. My father would not have missed.

Ruadan's low growl rumbled over the stone, his eyes on the angel as well. Piles of ash lay around us. It was only at this point that I realized my thoughts had been confused, muddled by my desperation to see my dad. Sometimes demons had feathered wings, and that was what this was.

Ruadan's icy magic whipped through the air as we stared up at the haloed demon, my lungs tight as a drum.

As the demon pulled another iron knife from a sheath, I got a glimpse of a purple amulet at his throat—a glowing lumen stone. Then, as he shifted away from the moon, a glimpse of red hair.

"Maddan," said Ruadan.

I took a step closer, gaping at him. "Maddan? Who gave you *wings?*"

CHAPTER 18

*H*e threw another knife, but I leapt forward and caught the hilt in midair.

"Good reflexes," he said. "You must be jealous that I can fly without creating an apocalypse."

I crossed my arms. "Um, actually, I can do it fine as long as I'm perpetually drunk." My mist soldiers still stood around me, waiting for my next orders. I could command them to tear Maddan to pieces, but I had so many questions for him before he died. "Okay, prince, how is it that you're flying, and how did you end up here?"

His wings beat the air. "Baleros asked me to keep an eye on you. He trusts me, now that I'm powerful. And as soon as I saw all the mist so far away from the Tower, I knew I'd found you. That's the problem with the mist armies, isn't it? Not very discreet. I flew toward the fog, and I thought, *there's my girl, torturing someone for information.* Again. And now I can tell Baleros where you are. He will make me one of his generals in no time."

"He already knows where we are." Ruadan gestured at all

the dusty piles. "He sent his army after us. The army died. You are completely useless."

Maddan's lip curled. "Right, well, I killed one of them before she gave you any valuable information. As I said. I'm an important asset."

I gaped at him. "Can we get back to the wings? Because what the hells?"

A bright blast of shadow magic crackled along Maddan's arm. "Mmmm, no. How about I kill you instead?"

A bone-shattering burst of shadow magic slammed me back into the stone wall. The magic seemed to freeze me from the inside out. Glacial emptiness pooled in my ribs, eating at me. My mind flickered with images of the shadow void—the skeletal trees, the jagged isolation.

Grunting, I rolled onto my hands and knees, muscles locking with the cold. The blast had knocked Ruadan back a bit, too. But since shadow magic was an intrinsic part of him, he absorbed it better.

From the rocky ground, I looked up at Maddan, who hovered like a dark angel before the moon. Violet shadow magic crackled over his body, icy cold. How had he acquired all this magic?

Wisps of magic curled off Ruadan, too. He summoned a ball of shadow magic in his palm, and he hurled it at Maddan.

Maddan rocketed back, but he recovered quickly. Within moments, bolts of shadow magic ignited the sky between them, flashing like lightning. As they fought each other, shadow magic electrified the air.

"*Evell dispennior,*" I said, and my mist soldiers melded together into an enormous bird. The creature swooped for him—but just before his beak clamped down on Maddan's head, the winged fae prince shadow-leapt away. The mist bird swirled and twisted back down to earth—silent sentinels once more, awaiting my commands.

Ruadan turned to me, his powerful body still crackling with magic. His eyes had darkened to pure black.

My muscles groaned, and I rubbed my shoulder. "I'm going to need a theory about what just happened, because that was bizarre. You got any ideas about how Maddan got wings?"

"Somehow, he's been in the void for a long time. The shadow void transformed him into a demon. The Maddan we just saw there is not the same as the Maddan you last knew."

"I have so many questions, I don't even know where to start." I rubbed my eyes. "Okay, I have one. I just saw him two days ago, minus the wings. How could it be that he's been in the void for a long time?"

"Time can pass differently there. Two days here could have been decades there. I doubt he went in willingly. His father probably forced him into the void in the hopes of getting a more useful son."

"Right. Okay, second of all, did Nyxobas make this happen?"

"Yes."

I really hated Ruadan's grandfather at this point. "Why would he give that walking cold sore more power?"

Ruadan cocked his head. "Have you wondered why Baleros has vampires working for him?"

I hugged myself, still cold from the shadow magic. "He always had vampires in the arena, but it *is* odd, considering he had committed his soul to Emerazel. The goddess of fire and the god of night are ancient enemies. They're not usually working on the same side."

"And yet, somehow, he's amassing shadow creatures on

his side. For whatever reason, Nyxobas is doing him favors. Nyxobas turned Maddan into a demon."

Demented Mike's words rang in my head. *The gods are hungry for souls, and they care for nothing else.*

I glanced at the moon. "The vampire I just interrogated said something about a ring. And a cage. Baleros gave Nyxobas a magic ring. Does that mean anything to you? A ring cage?"

Ruadan stared at me, eyes dark as jet. "A soul cage."

"What?"

"It's an object—like a ring or a stone—that's full of thousands of souls. They're extremely rare. They're the most powerful currency when bargaining with a god. With a soul cage, you can get a powerful ally. At least for a time."

The gods only care about one thing.... "Bloody hells. We don't even know what favors he's asked for. We have no idea what to expect." I thrust my fingers into my hair. "Maddan said that Baleros had a powerful ally on his side. I guess now we know who it is." My stomach was still in knots.

"What else did the vampires say?" asked Ruadan.

I nodded at one of the piles of ash, though I had no idea who was who at this point. "She said Baleros is in a church."

"Good. Okay. It's a start. But there are almost fifty churches within the square mile in the City, and several hundred in London as a whole."

We'd have to find Baleros later. Aenor came first. "You know what? Let's get this Skin Flayer woman first, and we will narrow down the churches later. We still need to get to my dad, or we won't have any Shadow Fae left to help us capture Baleros." I turned to my mist army, and I dismissed them with a single fae word. *"Distronnor."*

They wafted away, light puffs of smoke in the night. The Institute was vulnerable and needed the protection more than I did right now.

C.N. CRAWFORD

"Are you ready?" asked Ruadan.

I nodded, and we shadow-leapt over to the trap door Ruadan had opened. From there, we peered down into the tunnel. A faint, golden glow lit earthen walls. Ruadan was the first to jump into the trap door, his sword still drawn. He landed hard on the dirt floor, then beckoned for me to follow.

I scooted over the edge and jumped in after him, turning to face the source of light. We couldn't see much from here, and particles of dirt hung in the air. A cackling noise filled the dank tunnel, and the sound sent a shiver up my spine. Gripping our weapons, we marched toward the source of the light until the tunnel opened into a cavernous, earthen room.

On the far side, a woman with white hair sat in front of an aged television set, laughing. Two black cats dozed in her lap.

I had a feeling *this* wasn't Aenor. She smelled faintly of mold and soil, and little else. My first instinct was that these were guards of some kind—demonic creatures in disguise.

My hands started to sweat, paranoia spiking as I surveyed the room. *Calm yourself, Liora.* I was ready to stab this lady just because Baleros had trained me to kill first and ask questions later. I risked killing not only an innocent woman, but the person who could tell us where to find Aenor.

I loosened my grip on my sword. I was free from Baleros's influence now. I cocked my head, studying the woman.

She'd fashioned her nightgown into a sort of bowl, out of which she was eating sugar cereal mixed with what looked like small finger bones. Apart from the cats, the television, and an old pair of clogs on the floor, the room was just earth walls and floor.

Behind her ragged armchair, an aged door stood set into the wood. Like she was guarding it.

I cleared my throat. "Excuse me, do you know—"

She grunted, then pointed a bony finger at the television. "Don't interrupt my stories."

"We're looking for Aenor, Flayer of Skins," said Ruadan.

She popped a finger bone in her mouth. "Not me. I'm Karen, Watcher of Television. And you're interrupting the best parts."

After the night we'd had, I was all out of patience. "My name is Liora, Eviscerator of Those Who Don't Answer My Bloody Questions."

Ruadan put a steadying hand on my arm, and I felt soothing magic skim up my bicep. I narrowed my eyes at him. *Don't try to calm my anger. It's my oldest friend.*

Then, I let out a steadying breath. I wasn't Baleros's pawn anymore.

Ruadan's magic snaked over the room, almost as a warning. "You're Aenor's guard."

"Got that right." She crunched the cereal. "No one gets past me."

My fingers twitched on my hilt, and I glanced at the door just behind her. But it was Ruadan who spoke as he drew his sword from its sheath. Thick, dark vampire blood dripped off the blade onto the floor, and the cats began to stir in her lap, hackles raised.

"We're running out of time," said Ruadan, his voice laced with steel. "And we need to speak to Aenor, now. I don't want to have to hurt you."

This time, it was my turn to put a hand on Ruadan's arm, stilling his fury. "Wait," I whispered. What if she was just a frail old human woman with her cats?

She narrowed her eyes at the television. "No one's speaking to Aenor tonight," she grumbled. "Get out of here before I get cranky."

Ruadan shot me a furious glare. I'd interrupted his terri-fying demigod flow. "I will kill you if I have to," he added.

"You can stop grandstanding and showing off!" she barked. "You're about to forfeit your souls."

Oh, *shit.* What?

Her jaw unhinged, dropping open to reveal a chasm. The sound of a thousand tormented screams rose from her gullet, vibrating around my skull, then the room went silent once more. Her dark eyes were wide with fury.

The scream had transfixed me in place. Already, I could feel my body hollowing out, emptiness carving through me.

Bloody hells, Karen.

CHAPTER 19

*J*ust then, the door creaked open, and a voice called out, "Karen! I told you to send them through."

Karen snorted. "These two monsters?"

"Yes," the female voice said from the other room. "I've been waiting for them."

The TV reception crackled and sputtered. Karen reached down to throw a clog at the television set. She burst into laughter again, stuffing her mouth with sugar cereal and finger bones.

I turned to see what was so hilarious, disturbed to find that it was a PSA about drug addiction, featuring a man convulsing on the floor with a syringe sticking out of his arm.

She giggled. Then, without taking her gaze from the screen, she said, "Aenor's through there. Waiting, apparently. You can go on."

I stepped around the bits of cereal and bones on the floor to get to the door, and I squeezed past her armchair.

I pulled open the door to reveal a shop filled with shelves

of herbs, shrunken heads, and other unsettling curiosities. A rough-hewn counter stood by the far wall, its surface cluttered with bell jars of taxidermy animals and gnarled trinkets. But my eye was really drawn to the girl standing in the center of the shop.

Her pale blue hair draped over narrow shoulders and a tank top. She was hula-hooping in jean shorts and high heels. With her large, dark eyes and heart-shaped face, she seemed far too innocent for the eerie-looking tattoos all over her body. Her hips moved rhythmically to a crackling Elvis record. *Suspicious Minds*, specifically. Not what I'd been expecting. Gorgeous, tan skin, like a tiny goddess.

"We're looking for Aenor, Flayer of Skins," I began. "Scourge of the Wicked," I added, though it was probably not necessary. How many Aenor Skin Flayers could there be?

She blew an enormous pink chewing-gum bubble and popped it. The hula-hooping continued. "That's me."

I shot a quick look at Ruadan, but I could hardly see him. He was pulling his indistinct trick, coming in unnoticed.

"You're Aenor?" I asked.

"Yeah. I thought I saw you coming in one of my scrying mirrors. As it happens, I need to cut a deal with the Shadow Fae. Karen was supposed to let you past. She gets confused when she's watching her stories."

I'd been so fixated on Aenor that I nearly hadn't noticed the hearts nailed to the wall—desiccated, each one with a nail through the center. By their size, some looked human, and others looked demon or fae.

I bit my lip. "You sell hearts?"

"Yeah. *Men's* hearts." Just like that. Like it needed no other explanation beyond their gender. *Nothing untoward here. The owners of these organs had Y chromosomes, so obviously it's all above board.*

As she hula-hooped, she toyed with a silver locket around her neck.

"Right. Great. So—" I glanced at Ruadan again, hoping to convey with the arching of a single eyebrow that he needed to let me handle this, because this chick was crazy, and she hated blokes. I had no idea if he understood the gesture, since I couldn't see his face.

"Who are you?" she asked. Her accent was American.

I cleared my throat, now even more certain that I should disguise my identity until I knew more. What was a normal-sounding, believable pseudonym?

"My name," I began, "is … Dr. Margery T. Beaglehole."

Nope. Not that. Frustrated, I pinched the bridge of my nose, and I was pretty sure I could hear Ruadan sighing behind me.

"Yeah, that's not your name," said Aenor. "Adonis might have killed loads of people with his mind, but he'd never be cruel enough to name his kid Margery Beaglehole."

I stared at her. So, the jig was up. "How did you know I'm related to him?"

She finally stopped hula-hooping, letting the plastic ring drop to the floor. "Where's the guy you were with? The big demi-fae shadow demon? I saw him in the scrying mirror."

"Here." Ruadan chose that moment to appear, his eyes obsidian black, muscles tensed.

"Holy crap." Her pupils dilated for a moment, chest flushing so fast it was nearly imperceptible. Then, her gaze shuttered, and her lip curled in a sneer. She actually *snarled* at him like a wild animal.

I stepped in front of him protectively. "You can't have his heart. It's staying in his chest."

"He's a heartbreaker." She looked rattled, and she crossed behind the counter. "Do you know that?"

"We have been over that. So, back to the task at hand—how did you know I was Adonis's daughter?"

"You look like him. He's an old friend." She looked the same age as me, but she was obviously much older.

"I'm looking for him," I said, still giving away as little as I could. "Do you know anything?"

She touched the locket around her neck again. "I'm not real good with men, you know?"

I glanced at the dried hearts. "Is that so?"

"Most men are selfish, abusive, murderous assholes. Adonis was different. I mean, sure, he was the Horseman of Death." Another pink bubble popped. "But he didn't mean to kill people. He actually cared about people. He saved my life, once. And after that, we stayed friends. He actually listened to me. Sometimes it was really trivial shit. 'Oh, I had a hard time breaking a bone demon's ribs to get his heart out today.' Other times it was, like, existential dread. You know? Anyway, he's a good listener."

"Right. I remember. Vaguely." My instincts told me she was telling the truth.

"When the apocalypse started kicking off and all the other horsemen showed up," she went on, "I started to get worried about him. That's why he gave me this locket." She opened it up, but the glass inside appeared murky. "I could see him in it, just to make sure he was okay. That way, I'd know his curse hadn't taken effect, and I'd check on him when he was in Eden—just little glimpses of him. But a couple of weeks ago, he just disappeared from my locket. I don't know what happened to him."

My stomach fell. "How could he be gone? The worlds have been closed. He was locked in Eden. Only someone with a World Key can open the worlds. Baleros doesn't have a World Key."

"Baleros?"

"The man who's been spreading disease," I replied. "Rotten to the core. A festering sore on London's arse. He's—"

Ruadan touched my arm. "She gets the idea."

I inhaled deeply through my nose. "He's a bad man. Former slave master and would-be tyrant. He's after the World Key on Ruadan's chest. He spread plague to the knights of the Institute using the Unholy Grail. Now we need my dad to help cure them."

She cocked her head. "If you're his daughter, you must have some of his powers."

I nodded. "Right, but they kill people. Anyway, how could my father disappear from a locked world? He had no way out."

"I'm sure he's still there," she said. "But something happened to him to make him ... unseeable. I have no idea what." She leaned over the counter, her eyes suddenly intense, and she gripped my arms. "He can't die, can he? He once told me he can't die. Unless your mom kills him."

I bit my lip. "I doubt she did that."

She pointed at Ruadan. "He's a seneschal from the Institute. He has a World Key. Why can't he get you into Eden?"

"We did go, and we found no one. Just graves. But I'm pretty sure it was glamoured," I said. "It was like a facade. There was just one tiny detail that was different. And under that detail, I found the note to come find you."

She nodded slowly. "Ah. Good. Well, I can help you get through glamour. That's probably why he sent you to me. I'm desperate to know where your dad is, and I've been wanting to strike a deal with the Shadow Fae."

"Good." Ruadan's icy presence filled the room. "That's settled. We'll go now."

She narrowed her eyes at him. "You know it's after

midnight, right? I mean, I'm a night owl, but why does this need to happen right now?"

I leaned on the countertop, urgency tensing my muscles. I stared into her dark eyes. "It needs to happen right now, Aenor, because there's a plague spreading in the city of London. The person who is causing all this wants to take over the world with an army full of demons. And the knights of the Institute have to stop him. Except they've got the Plague, and they're about to die."

She arched an eyebrow. "I'm not really a fan of the Institute, is the thing. I used to have a shop above ground like a normal heart-selling fae. Since the Institute took control, I've literally had to go underground. I live in constant fear that one of you will kill me. I'm not saying I want them to die, but...." She shrugged.

Ruadan's dark magic thickened. "You said you wanted something from the Shadow Fae in return for your help. Is that what you're building up to?"

She blew a strand of pale blue hair out of her eyes. "Yeah. I want protection. If I help you, I want to live freely in London. I don't want any Shadow Fae stabbing me with iron just because I'm not in a locked realm like a good little girl."

"Agreed," said Ruadan. "But you know that if the current knights die, they'll be replaced by new knights. And those knights won't honor this agreement. So we need Adonis to heal them now."

She smacked her hand on the countertop. "Then I guess we'd better find him." Without taking her eyes off me, she bellowed, "Cora! Get your butt out here. We've got some witchery to do."

A minute later, a girl with peach-colored hair stumbled into the room through a beaded curtain, rubbing her eyes. Like Aenor, tattoos covered her pale skin. "Are you kidding me, Aenor? This had better be important. In my dream, I was *just* about to kiss this super hot incubus. I think he was a demigod—" She blinked, staring at Ruadan, then me. "Who are these people?"

Aenor pointed at Ruadan. "Well, he's an incubus, for one thing. And I think possibly a demigod."

Cora stared at him. "I was just joking. I hate incubi. I mean, I find you repulsive." Then she looked away, muttering something that sounded like, "Too much."

"He has a World Key," added Aenor. "And he is promising us amnesty from the Shadow Fae in return for our help."

"The both of you, then," said Ruadan.

Aenor straightened. "The both of us require amnesty. Permanently."

"Fine."

Cora was staring at his chest, where the World Key glowed. "Bloody hells." She rubbed the sleep out of her eyes. "Just so I'm clear, we don't need to attack the Shadow Fae?"

"No." Aenor drummed her fingernails on the countertop. "I know her dad. They need our help."

"At this hour?" said Cora. "Why?"

I met her gaze. "At the risk of sounding dramatic, you're going to help us save the world."

"And more importantly," added Aenor, "that whole bit about amnesty."

Cora heaved a sigh. "Fine. What do we need to do?"

Aenor turned away from the counter. "We need to travel to another world and disintegrate its magical defenses. Let's get our things together, shall we?"

CHAPTER 20

*I*t was only a few more minutes before we were deep in the watery portal, swimming our way to the surface.

I climbed out of the portal, then whirled around to help Aenor and Cora out. I gripped their arms, hauling them up. Both of them had their own bug-out bags now, full of their own witchy stuff. Probably waterlogged hearts of men.

Aenor dropped her sodden bag on the earth, catching her breath, and Cora hunched over with her hands on her knees as she recovered.

Ruadan called up a ball of silver light that illuminated the clearing a bit more. While the two witches caught their breath, I surveyed the woods around me.

It looked so much like the home I remembered. Moonlight streamed between the leaves, and the wind rushed over groaning boughs of ancient oaks. To my left, outside the wood's edge, were the village homes, silent and still as graves.

I wrapped my arms around myself, shivering. I knew the desolation of this landscape was just an illusion, but the forest's quiet felt wrong. The only sound here was the low song of the wind through the trees. It was like I was standing in the hollow carapace of my former home.

I glanced at Aenor, who'd started pulling things out of her witch bag to lay on the moss. So far, she'd yanked out a demon heart, a few bones, wax candles, a jar of salt, and a few jars of herbs.

"Can I help?" I asked.

"No," said Aenor. "Just stay out of the way while Cora collects a crow."

I glanced at Cora, who was making a cooing sound, holding her hands up to the tree branches. I stared as a dark bird fluttered onto her finger. Cora held onto its body, whispering into its ear. The crow's eyes closed as it relaxed. Then, she released the bird above us. It flapped over our heads, the sound of its wings oddly loud.

As she did that, Aenor poured the salt in a circle around us, muttering quietly in Angelic. She placed four candles in the center of the circle, then snapped her fingers to light the candles.

Aenor looked at me and curled a finger to beckon me to her. "Everyone come closer. Join hands with us."

"We need all the power we can get," added Cora.

Aenor's blue hair—and mine, too—wafted in the air. The hair on the back of my arms was also standing on end as the air charged with magic.

Cora's peach hair snaked around her head as if she were underwater. She closed her eyes. "This glamour is powerful. Can you feel it?"

Ruadan stepped into the circle of magic, his pale hair lifting in the breeze. He traced his finger through the air, leaving a trail of dark magic that glimmered faintly. "It's not just fae magic. There's night magic here, too."

What on earth? "How? Neither of my parents could use

night magic. We had no night demons in Eden. Are you sure?"

He shot me a sharp look, which I quickly interpreted as *I am a demigod of the night; do not question my knowledge of night magic.*

Aenor held out her hands to either side. "I guess we'll find out when we break through the glamour."

My entire body felt taut as a bowstring, buzzing with tension. Nothing about this seemed right—the night magic, my father's mysterious disappearance from Aenor's locket. I couldn't escape the feeling that something terrible had happened.

"Hang on," said Cora, pulling her hands away from the circle. "I was a little sleepy before, but now that the ice water portal has woken me up, please explain again why we're about to open a world with the Horseman of Death in it. Is it just me, or is a Horseman of Death someone you're better off leaving alone?"

I glared at her. "It's just you. He's not dangerous."

"Explain," she shot back.

"Okay," I said. "The horsemen were all born with a curse. It was an Angelic spell known as a seal. If the seals were opened, the horsemen turned evil. If my father's seal had opened, he would have carried out his true purpose—to kill nearly everyone on earth using his death magic. But his seal was never opened. The curse never took effect."

"Liora's mother took the spell off him completely," added Aenor. "She used her magic to do it. She had some kind of insanely powerful fae magic at her fingertips. And that's why we're going to need all the power we can get to break through the magical protections she put up."

"Okay." Cora held out her hands to either side, signaling that we were supposed to start.

I grasped Cora's hand in one of mine, and Ruadan's in the other.

"Wait." Cora jerked her hand away, and she stared at Aenor. "You said he disappeared from your locket, right? What if he changed? Maybe the curse took hold after all. Don't you know the prophecy of the gods?" Her hair whipped wildly around her head, and a ferocious wind rushed through the forest. "*I looked, and behold, an ashen horse.*" Leaves blew off the tree branches, rushing around us in a vortex. "*And he who rode it had the name Death, and Hell followed him.*"

As she spoke, my skin went cold, and my shoulder blades ached to release their wings.

"We get the idea, Cora," said Aenor.

But Cora wasn't finished. She closed her eyes. "*And power was given to them—to kill with sword, and with hunger, and with death, and with the beasts of the earth.*"

I felt like my soul was rising from the grave. As she spoke, I felt overwhelmed by the urge to unleash death all over the world, followed by the urge to dull my rage with whiskey. But I was fresh out. My gaze flicked to the moon. Red tinged its surface, as if thick blood were spilling across its surface. Then, the illusion disappeared again.

"Why are you quoting this ancient prophecy?" Ruadan's eyes had darkened, the temperature chilling around us.

Death magic still whispered over my skin. *As I walk the earth, grass and wheat turns to ash before me....*

"Because the prophecy hasn't yet come to pass," said Cora. "But it will. The gods always make good on their prophecies. And they always have their way. We're just their pawns."

Nyxobas's words knelled in my mind: *Ruadan dies at the end of all this.*

"Bollocks," I said. "Gods' prophecies are a load of shite.

They don't always come true." I had nothing logical or factual to back up my argument—just my own iron will.

Cora made a sign warding off blasphemy.

"We don't have time for a theological argument right now," said Ruadan. "You have heard about the Plague spreading, right? It has spread beyond the Tower walls, and it will get worse. If the Institute falls, and if Baleros gets his hands on the World Key, he will conscript armies of demons to serve him. Then, death will truly stalk the earth."

"That's the thing about prophecies," I said. "They're vague. Could be anything. We still have free will." Despite my rising fears, I tried to be logical. "Are you going to help us or not?"

"She'll help us," Aenor said, cutting in. "She's a religious nut, but she mostly just wants the opportunity to say 'I told you so' if she happens to be right."

"Opportunity granted," I said testily. "Let's begin."

We held hands once more. Cora and Aenor began chanting. Above our heads, the crow cawed loudly, flapping its wings. The candle flames rose higher, casting wavering golden light over the oak grove.

The prophecy Cora quoted rang in my mind. *Hell followed him....*

Around us, magic whipped along with the breeze, rushing and tingling over my skin. Ruadan's energy blended with the spell's magic, and his power felt cold and silky on my body.

I am the dark rot that starts in your fingertips....

Above us, the crow cawed, and the winds picked up, blowing fallen leaves in a vortex around us. The candle flames rose to the height of our chests now. Something had to be working. At any moment, I could be rushing into the real Eden, embracing my parents.

A powerful magic erupted around us. Then, I stared as the world around us shimmered and the glamour fell away. A few lights burned in the village windows. *Home.*

My heart leapt, cheeks warming. "We're here," I whispered.

I pulled away from the circle, taking a step toward the village.

"Be cautious, Liora," said Ruadan.

It was like I felt his voice inside me instead of hearing it out loud, and I paused to turn back to him. His eyes were on me, his warm protectiveness washing over me. He looked at me like he'd been cursed and I was his salvation. He was right. How could I have ever doubted him?

I turned away from him, heading back to my old home. I broke into a run once more, tearing down the path for my house. Warm lights beamed from windows onto the dirt roads. My feet pounded over the ground, and I sprinted past the crooked homes, the temple, the grassy common—beautifully, wonderfully free from grave markers, not a stone in sight.

Then, I careened toward my old home, where a light burned in the kitchen window.

Mum. Dad....

I screeched to a halt before their door, jolted by the awareness that barging into their home might alarm them.

I caught my breath, and my heart slammed against my ribs. Then, I knocked gently on the door. When there was no answer after a few moments, I rapped again, a little louder. Silence greeted me.

I turned, looking across the town green, where I could see the witches walking cautiously.

I shifted to the window, cupping my hands to peer inside. Light burned in a lantern, and a few plates were set out in the kitchen. Signs of life. Where were my parents, though?

I couldn't wait any longer, and I decided to try the door. My parents *never* locked the house. Why would they? We knew everyone in Eden.

I turned the knob, and the door creaked open.

Lanterns, lit with oil, hung from the ceiling, bathing the room in gold. I rushed over to the fireplace, where I found the word *Bug* engraved, just as it should be. I ran my fingertips over it, unable to control the shaking.

"Dad?" I called out, my voice catching.

More silence greeted me.

I took in the space around me, trying to rein in my wild emotions.

Our living room was combined with the kitchen—a stove and fireplace on one side, sofas and a rug on the other. A hall at the back led to the bedrooms and the library and bath upstairs. They could be upstairs, I supposed.

"Dad?" I asked again, quietly. Apprehension danced up my spine. Something was wrong here, and it took me a few moments to figure out what it was.

Why had my parents left the lanterns on at this hour? It was the middle of the night, and they didn't leave them on when they were upstairs sleeping.

I sniffed the air. The room smelled musty. No, worse than musty. It smelled *rotten*.

My heart skipped a beat. Something was definitely wrong in Eden.

CHAPTER 21

I turned to find Ruadan behind me, sniffing the air as well. He frowned.

I was about to scream at him to get out of here—that if my dad found him, everyone would die. Except my dad didn't seem to be here.

"Something's wrong," he said. "The scent of fae is too faint. I smell you, and the two witches … the rest of it is faint. And the smell of rotten food is powerful." He peered out the window. "Cora and Aenor are checking on some houses across the way."

My chest clenched. "I know. Let me just look upstairs."

"Perhaps you should do that alone."

He spoke the truth. If Ruadan burst into my parents' bedroom while they were sleeping, the wave of death my father would unleash would kill anyone within a fifty-mile radius.

"Yeah, you might want to search discreetly outside, doing your invisible Wraith thing. I can handle my empty house."

"Call to me if you need me." Ruadan disappeared in a blur of dark magic.

I drew my sword, stepping into the hallway. The floor creaked as I walked down its length, my heart thundering. I swallowed hard, standing outside my old room. The door was closed, and I turned the knob, inching it open. I caught my breath.

My parents had kept it *exactly* as I'd left it. The stuffed rabbit I'd loved—who I'd creatively named *Mr. Rabbit*—lay on my green velvet pillow. I was thirteen when I'd left, too old for soft toys, but I still slept with Mr. Rabbit every night until the day the world had ended.

An old pair of shorts and a shirt lay strewn across the floor where I'd left them. A baseball cap, my T-shirts, my trousers in a ball in the corner. The room was preserved like a museum of misery. While the rest of the house had been clean, a thick layer of dust covered the surfaces in this room. My parents hadn't touched a thing in here, like they could distill my essence just by leaving it untouched.

While I'd thought every day about how much I missed them, I'd never thought about how much they must have missed me. I hadn't been imagining what they'd gone through.

With stinging eyes, I crossed back into the hall, heading for the stairwell. I moved swiftly up the stairs, heading for their bedroom. The door was open a few inches, but it looked dark inside.

Holding my breath, I inched it open. Then, my chest constricted at the sight of another empty bedroom. Moonlight streamed over a tidy double bed and sleek furniture.

While my room had been preserved, this one looked different. A portrait of me, as I was at age twelve, hung on the wall. Short purple hair, my eyes wide open with an innocence I'd long since lost. The bed had been made, and I picked up one of the pillows. I smelled the myrrh scent of my father's magic, but it was faint.

A single, midnight feather lay on the floor by the bed.

I crouched down to pick it up. I twirled it between my fingers, and the silver streaks in the feather caught in the moonlight streaming through the window. Breathtakingly beautiful, just like he was. I shoved the feather into my pocket as a keepsake.

My blood roaring, I rushed to the closet door, and hope began to bloom. Clothes from both my parents hung on hangers—my mum's shimmering dresses, my father's sober black clothes. They looked new. They'd been here recently, I was sure.

I turned back to the bed, blood pumping hard. I crawled onto the mattress, straining my eyes in the faint light. A single strand of cherry-red hair lay across the pillow.

"Mum." I plucked the hair off the pillow, feeling slightly like a weirdo. But it was my one tenuous connection to her now.

Maybe they'd run to hide because they'd seen us coming? I glanced back at the short-haired, wide-eyed, full-cheeked girl in the portrait. They'd hardly recognize me now. A gladiator, covered in scars.

I felt completely uneasy in here. The hair on my nape stood on end. I had the strangest feeling that I was being watched—a primal part of my brain warning me of danger.

But who was watching me? There didn't seem to be anyone here.

I searched one room after another—the library, bathroom, the guest room. Apart from my room, everything looked a bit changed—new furniture, new clothes. And no people. No matter what, my parents were just out of my reach, elusive. I felt like I was chasing smoke.

I gazed out one of the windows that overlooked my parents' garden. For just a moment, I thought I saw a pair of pale eyes glaring at me from the shrubs. In the next moment, they were gone again.

Adrenaline pounded through my blood. Who was out there?

I rushed back down to the kitchen, skin tingling again as the faintly rotten smell hit my nostrils. A clean set of plates lay on the wood table, along with bowls and spoons. A corked bottle of wine stood on the table, too.

I crossed to it and uncorked it, sniffing. It didn't smell terrible. When I drank it, it tasted acidic. If I had to guess, it was a few weeks old.

I crossed to the fireplace, where a lidded pot hung. It smelled stronger here. I pulled the copper lid off the pot, and an acrid smell hit me—burnt, rotten meat. I couldn't even tell what it had been originally, but it was now a charred mess, and it looked as if it had been left there for weeks. I retched.

So they had been about to eat dinner, and then they'd just disappeared, letting the food char? How was this possible?

I rushed out of the house, into the cool night air. "Ruadan!" I called out. I wasn't trying to be quiet anymore. Now, I was certain my parents were gone from Eden.

Ruadan flitted over to me in a whirlwind of shadow magic.

A few houses down, Aenor and Cora crossed out of a home. Aenor shrugged.

"There's no one here," said Ruadan. "Anywhere in Eden."

"We just found a load of half-eaten, rotten food and clothes left out," said Cora.

"Everywhere, it looks like the people who lived here just disappeared, mid-dinner."

I shook my head. "How is this possible? The worlds were locked. Only a seneschal like Ruadan could open them."

"Or...." Ruadan's dark magic lashed the air around him. "Or a god. It's the gods' power that we drew on to create the locked worlds. A god could toy with it now." Ruadan traced his fingertips through the air, and shimmering night magic followed in the wake of his stroke. "Perhaps Nyxobas toyed with this world."

"The night magic..." said Cora. "Why would Nyxobas open this world?"

"Godsdamn it!" I started pacing. "This is one of the favors that Nyxobas is doing for Baleros. We think that Baleros gave him a soul cage. A magic ring."

"A soul cage," Aenor repeated. "You could have mentioned we were up against someone with a soul cage before we came in here."

Ruadan met my gaze steadily, and I could feel the rage curling off him like smoke. "The gods only care about one thing."

"Souls," Cora finished his thought. "And the gods always win."

Ruadan swore under his breath.

I threaded my fingers through my hair. Anger flooded me. "What if Baleros found a way to...." What if he'd killed everyone? I could hardly finish the thought. I was pacing furiously now, my mind racing. "No," I reassured myself, "Baleros wouldn't kill them. All those fae lives. Too wasteful." I was muttering to myself now, desperately trying to read into Baleros's thought processes. "No, that would be a waste. He's not a sadist just for fun, he finds a way to use people, doesn't he? Leverage, slavery ... living creatures have intrinsic value as long as he can use them...."

"Are you okay?" Aenor was looking at me with concern.

"I'm just trying to figure out what Baleros has done with my parents." I heaved a sigh. "And everyone else. I don't suppose you know any tracking spells?"

Aenor cocked her hip. "Yes, but I need something from the person, like a fingernail or a—"

"A feather?" I pulled the feather from my father's wing out of my pocket. It glinted silver in the moonlight.

"Exactly," said Aenor. "We'll need a few more things for the spell."

"Blood from a succubus," added Cora. "Ashes from a phoenix."

"And I'll have to burn the feather as part of the spell," said Aenor.

"I've got a strand of hair from my mum as well." My gaze darted between them defensively. "What? I missed them."

"They'll do, but we want to get out of this world before using them," said Ruadan. "I'll open the portal, and we can return to their bone shop."

Good. I didn't like it here anymore, and I couldn't escape the eerie feeling that I was being watched, that the primal part of my brain was warning me that something was amiss.

Ruadan backed away from us, then summoned his violet magic. His body glowed with gold.

I frowned at him. His gold and violet magic whipped the air around him, and the World Key glowed so brightly on his chest that it was beaming through his black shirt. Tension rippled off him, and violet magic crackled over the earth by his feet. Shadow magic, I thought.

I shivered. "Something wrong?" Normally, he'd just rip open a hole between the worlds without a second thought.

He opened his eyes, and shadows slid through them. "Yes. The portal isn't opening."

CHAPTER 22

*D*read coiled around my heart.

"If Baleros can get a god to open a world…" said Ruadan in a voice that chilled me.

"He can close it, too," Aenor finished his sentence. "Like a prison."

I clenched my fists so tight my fingernails pierced my palm.

"Stand back," said Ruadan.

I beckoned to the two witches. "Let's get far away from him. His magic is powerful."

As we walked away, Ruadan shadow-leapt across the green. Not far from the temple, his body glowed brightly with shadow magic and the gold of the World Key on his chest.

Then, a wave of magic erupted from his body, tearing along the earth and ripping up grass on the green. The force of it knocked me *hard* to the ground, and I grunted, rolling over. I coughed at the dirt clouding the air. I rose, dusting myself off. By my side, Aenor helped up Cora, muttering angrily as she did. Dirt and particles of leaves and glass clouded the air.

"Please tell me that opened the portal," I said, coughing into my arm.

"It did not open the portal," was Ruadan's somber response.

As the dust cleared, I could see magic crackling over the ripped-up soil and roots, but the ground was still closed over. I coughed into my arm again.

"Since Nyxobas used shadow magic to seal this," said Ruadan, "my own shadow magic is only adding to the shield. I think I just made it stronger."

"So we are just trapped here now," said Aenor.

Cora's pinkish hair snaked around her head, electrified by the shadow magic in the air. "Not to be a jerk, but this is what I meant when I said the gods always win. We live in their world, we play by their rules, and they don't give a single divine fuck about us. They always win, and we always lose."

"You're a right ray of sunshine, aren't you?" I said.

She narrowed her eyes. "Trust me on this."

"What about the one we came through? Will that still be open?"

Ruadan shook his head. "I can't feel it anymore. I think it closed up after we came through here."

"Let's check," said Aenor, already taking off, her pale blue hair trailing behind her tiny body.

I clenched my fists as I hurried after her. "So what is happening now? Baleros has a god doing his bidding permanently? He won't even need the World Key with that sort of power. He can just have Nyxobas do the work for him."

Ruadan shook his head as he stalked toward the forest's edge. "No. In return for thousands of souls, Nyxobas will do a favor or two for him. For a short time. He won't give him a

World Key, and he won't be permanently doing his bidding. Baleros wants to be able to open the worlds in order to harvest his armies, right?"

I nodded. "So he started with this world, because…." I bit my lip. "Well I don't know, exactly, but it must be linked to my father. We know Baleros is obsessed with spreading the plague. My father could do it if he feels enough emotional pain." Panic clawed at my heart. "What if Baleros wants to kill my mum, or torture her until my dad breaks? What if he—"

Ruadan touched my arm, brushing his knuckles over my bicep. His calming magic snaked over my body like a balm. "We don't know exactly what Baleros is thinking, and we may not figure it out until we find him. We have to take this one step at a time. The next step is getting out of here. Then we find your father using the tracking spell. We'll get through this."

"Right. Right." I wrung my hands. "One step at a time."

"Baleros has made one mistake," said Ruadan. "He's playing two gods against each other, making promises to both Nyxobas and Emerazel. I'm not sure how it will end, but it probably won't go well for him. You cannot serve two masters."

We walked in gloomy silence, slipping beyond the line of creaking oaks until we reached the forest portal—or, at least, the mossy soil where it had been. My stomach fell.

"Gone," said Ruadan. He traced his fingertips thorough the air, and violet shadow magic shimmered. Then, his pale eyes shifted to the two fae witches. "What gods do you serve?"

Aenor cocked her head. "What does that matter?"

That's when the feeling returned to me—the eyes on my back, watching us. Ruadan sensed it too, and he whirled, drawing his sword.

"You feel that, too?" I whispered, drawing my own sword. "The eyes watching us?"

"Yes," he said.

"I thought no one was here," Aenor said in a hushed voice. Blue magic swirled and crackled down her arm.

Ruadan nodded back to the forest's edge, signaling that we should move toward it. We walked quietly, looking all around us for the source of the threat. I tried to scent what we might be dealing with, but I only smelled the electrical scent of shadow magic among the forest's usual smells.

Ruadan sniffed the air again, and a low growl rumbled from his chest. The air grew colder around us. Glacial, even, and icy mist frosted in front of my face.

A growing sense of dread tightened my gut. We were trapped in Eden, and the one thing I knew for certain was that Baleros wanted Ruadan dead so he could rip the skin off his chest.

Baleros had trapped us here to die.

A flicker of movement caught my eye, and my fingers tightened on the hilt of my sword. We paused within the shadows of the forest's edge.

Across the clearing, near the rows of houses, a creature crawled out of one of the homes. He crept low to the ground with elongated movements. He looked vaguely human, except his body was emaciated, ribs sticking out, and his fingers were long and sharply pointed. His face had a slightly elongated, skeletal snout, and ivory antlers jutted from his head.

"What the hells?" I breathed.

"Shadow demons," Ruadan whispered. So *that's* why we couldn't smell them—they just smelled like all the other shadow magic around here.

More pale, gray eyes appeared from the shadows—dozens of them, and my legs started to shake with anticipation. The demons howled; a lonely, desolate sound that opened a pit in my stomach.

This was what I was made for—killing. This was where I felt comfortable. My wings tingled at my shoulder blades, and a dark smile curled my lips. *Come at me, you animals.*

As they started to run for us, I broke into a sprint to meet them, my sword ready.

I'll bury all of you in the earth. I'll rip your hearts from your bodies.

Magic flashed around me as Cora and Aenor began hurling their spells, blue and green igniting the air around us. When the magic struck the demons, they screamed—the sound was disturbingly human, agonized.

I reached the nearest demon, and I swung for him. I struck him through the neck, severing his spine. Battle fury surged in my bones, and I whirled.

Pivot, strike, carve.

I was moving fast enough that I kept them off me with the tip of my blade, swinging it in controlled arcs around me.

I glanced at Ruadan. His movements were breathtaking. Never was his divine nature more apparent than when he was fighting. Me? Not so graceful. I grunted, sweating, snarling—half animal. But I was delivering just as much death.

I scanned the surroundings. More gray eyes closing in on us. An army of them. My pulse roared.

So we were trapped in a locked world with an entire bloody legion of bestial demons hells-bent on killing us.

Bloodlust charged my body, increasing my speed as I fought them. But they were moving fast, too. A demon's claws raked at my back, drawing blood. They were all around me now, closing in. Another claw pierced my flesh, and it sparked something in me—a wild hunger. I wanted to taste blood.

A demon hand grabbed me from behind, claws digging into my throat.

"Grmmel margrr numen," one of them whispered in my ear. A demon tongue.

I grabbed him by the arm and flipped him over my shoulder, slamming him down on the earth. Then, I drove my sword through his neck.

Now, the world around me started to seem a little indistinct, the edges hazy. Still, I fought to keep my focus. I swung again, trying to keep up my speed. My swings were a little off now. What was happening to me?

Sparks danced before my eyes, and with each swing of the sword, silver trailed through the air.

This was not good.

I saw a gap in the demons around me, and I frantically cut my way through it, trying to fight my way out. I made a break for it and started sprinting. I was fighting to keep up my speed, but some kind of toxin seemed to be poisoning me.

Poison in the demons' claws.

I didn't make it far before they cornered me, isolating me from the others. I couldn't see Ruadan anymore, or the flashes of blue and green magic from the two witches.

As I tried to make my retreat, I realized I'd ended up near the rows of houses—only the buildings looked different now, like they were made of bone.

To my horror, the demons' faces began to shift. They were no longer the skeletal, elongated snouts of beasts—they were transforming into fae faces. Distinctly familiar faces that made my heart wither.

CHAPTER 23

*D*ozens of Baleroses surrounded me, smirking at me while I stumbled away from them. Now, the air smelled of roses, that sickeningly sweet smell.

"Losing control, are you?" said one of the demons, an infuriating smile curling his lips.

I staggered closer to him, swinging for him with my sword. I missed.

The laughter of a dozen Baleroses rang around me. I was dizzy now, and the slave masters were toying with me.

I fell back through a door, landing hard on a wood floor. Was I back in my parents' house?

A Baleros leapt for me—his face was that of my old master, but his hands sharpened into lethal claws. Metal clanged on wood, and I knew I'd lost my sword.

Baleros smiled above me, controlled and lethal. "You were born evil, Liora, angel of death. Born to kill. Flowers wilt around you, grass turns to ash. Your breath is a toxin that poisons the earth. Sparrows fall from the sky and the trees turn to bone. You are an abomination on this earth; a festering, rotting monster, repugnant under your skin. You would kill your own kin." Claws raked down the front of my chest, drawing blood. "You kill those you love."

I punched him hard, again and again in the jaw. He unleashed that scream again—the one that sounded half human, half beast. His clawed hands gripped my throat, squeezing, piercing the flesh.

More poison.

"A monster like you," he whispered, "should stay in its cage."

Darkness slammed into me. I wanted blood, flesh, bones. I wanted to crush them into the earth.

And I would.

My voice came out choked. "A monster like me should stay in its cage." Rage flared hot though my muscles, and I punched him hard in the face again, cracking his jaw, breaking bones. "But I got out."

Fury burned through my body—and with it, strength. I was a hurricane of vengeance, and my enemies were all around me.

I punched him again, hard, and the creature fell off me. I snatched my sword off the floor. That dark, cold euphoria snaked through my body as I grabbed the hilt.

The demons were right—I was born to kill.

Flowers wilt before me.

Bollocks. I needed some alcohol to stop myself from murdering my allies.

Instinctively, my demonic attackers were already backing away as death magic started to snake off my body. My beautiful, dark wings erupted from my shoulder blades. As they did, I snatched the wine off my parents' table, chugging it down, ignoring the sharp vinegary taste.

I dropped the empty wine bottle and gripped my sword with both hands.

Despite my buzz, I felt steady on my feet as I moved

around the room, slaughtering one demon after another. My sword cut through their spines, severing their lives instantly. I no longer felt dizzy or off-balance.

Their deaths filled me with power, my body growing gloriously strong.

I was a fomoire in my own way. Ruadan fed off heartbreak; I fed off death. And right now, I felt positively glowing.

Pivot, strike, carve.

Demon blood and gore stained my parents' floor. In the back of my mind, I knew my mum would be furious. But I kept slaughtering, kept hammering them with my blade.

I moved in a maelstrom of brutality until every creature —every freakish, Baleros-headed demon in my parents' home—lay broken on the floor. I stood over them, catching my breath. It was at that point I realized the illusion had faded. They no longer looked like my old gladiator master— just ordinary freakish demons.

In any case, my childhood home had become a mausoleum of my enemies. Right now, I liked it that way.

Sword in hand, I crossed to the door and stalked outside.

I will take more lives tonight. Their heads will rot on spikes. I will create a garden of death.

Colored magic sparked in the air across Eden, electrifying it with blue and green, the air tinged with the scent of brine. My lips tasted of salt.

Ecstasy lit me up as my wings lifted me into the air, moonlight washing over me as my flight carried me closer to the mob of demons. I dodged the sparks of blue and green magic as I flew. The demons had surrounded the fae witches.

I'll feed the soil with their blood.

I angled my wings, flying lower. Blood dripped from my sword. I attacked from above, cutting through necks, their skulls. I'd fertilize this beautiful fae earth with the gore from their bodies.

Fools sacrifice to the earthly gods. Death is the greatest power of them all. I landed on the soil and whirled into action. *Break their bodies—feed the earth. All fall before me.*

As death power filled me, imbuing every muscle with strength, I became insatiable. I wanted to drive every living creature into the earth, crush each of them to dust. Around me, I no longer saw the demons' faces, only their beating hearts. Life I needed to crush. Hearts that must stop. With every ruptured aorta, another wild thrill of power rippled through my chest.

Now, I'd snuffed so many lives out that there were hardly any left. Gods, I wanted *more*. More still lungs, more severed heads. More blood on my blade.

There—a most beautiful heart beating, so large and healthy. I needed to rip the thing in half. All beautiful things must die. I'd crush it like a rose in my fist.

A name pierced the fog of my bloodlust, and my movements stilled. Death magic started to ripple along my arms, down my fingertips, and I yearned to unleash it, to slaughter every living creature. How glorious it would feel to kill them all … every last moth and hummingbird. I'd crush the sparrows in my fist and wring the blood from their bodies, grind their bones to dust.

"Death is my name," I snarled. "All fall before me."

"Liora!" That beautiful, rich, deep voice stroked my skin, calming me. Silky magic brushed over my body. My body was shaking, legs trembling, but that soothing magic warmed me from the inside out.

The heart—the one I'd longed to stop with my powers—still beat. And now, I became aware of the body around it. The powerful fae body, the one marked with savage tattoos.

The arms that would always protect me—violet eyes and pale gold hair.

"Ruadan," I breathed.

All the death power rushed out of my body like a wild river and nausea replaced it. I hunched over on the ground, on my hands and knees. Dark blood soaked the soil from all the demons I'd just killed.

I choked down my urge to vomit, mastering control of myself once more. Then, I lifted my eyes to search the battle-ground around me.

But the battle was over. Only Ruadan remained, and the two fae witches, peeking out from behind the trunks of oak trees. Their brightly colored magic still electrified their bodies.

Aenor stepped out from behind the oak, her dark eyes wide. "That was … interesting."

Ruadan leaned down. Holding my elbow, he helped me rise to my feet, his magic still soothing me. As it whispered over my skin, it took some of the shaking out of my limbs, the cramping out of my muscles. My wings had disappeared, and strangely, their absence felt like a loss.

I surveyed the land around me. Broken bodies littered the ground—severed spines, streams of demon blood seeping into the earth.

"You're a formidable ally," said Ruadan. "Dangerous, but formidable."

I pointed at his heart, catching my breath. "Sorry about the, um— I almost killed you."

Tentatively, Cora stepped out from behind the tree. "So *that's* what people mean by 'orgy of violence.' I'd never had the visual before. I could have done without it in my brain, honestly."

I gripped my stomach. "Are you really judging me? One of you goes by the nickname *Flayer of Skins*."

Aenor shrugged. "I do keep things tidy, though." Then, she crouched down and pulled out a knife. She started to carve out one of the demon's hearts. "This will fetch a pretty penny."

"Who do you plan on selling it to?" asked Cora. "The corpses of the other demons? There's no one else here, and we remain trapped."

I looked at Ruadan. "Any ideas how to open the world beyond what we've tried?"

He scrubbed a hand over his mouth. "My magic only strengthened the barrier between the worlds. It melded with my grandfather's. Our magic is one and the same. We need the magic of other gods to break through it. And it has to be powerful."

Aenor gripped the bleeding demon heart. "Good thing you have us, then. I serve Dagon, the sea god."

Cora raised a hand. "Storm god."

"I can chant the Angelic spell to open the world," said Ruadan, "but I'll need your magic to break its bonds."

Apprehension tingled over my skin once more, the hair rising on my nape, and I glanced at the forest's edge. Ice slid through my bones. There, between the trunks, thousands of pale eyes gleamed with shadow magic. A legion of demons surrounded us, ready to strike again.

I swallowed hard. "You might want to do that now, ladies."

Aenor looked into the woods, her pupils dilating. "Oh, dear."

"I'm not going to be able to kill them all," I said. A deep fatigue had spread through my bones. "I'll do what I can while you work your magic."

"Careful, Liora." Ruadan's voice, again like balm around my body.

Sword in my hand, I stalked toward the forest's edge. "Just open the portal as fast as you can."

From behind me, Ruadan's Angelic chants filled the air. The air ignited with storm and sea magic—salt and the scent of brine floated on the breeze. Lightning cracked the sky, clouds roiling overhead. A heavy rain started to fall. The two witches were strange creatures, but I'd quickly come to love them and their magic.

The first line of demons rushed for me, tearing through the forest, snarling. Luckily, there weren't many yet. This time, I knew better than to let them get their claws into me. The tip of my sword kept them at bay. Adrenaline sapped away the weakness in my bones.

The ground trembled, thundering with the sound of the oncoming horde of demons. A few favors, Ruadan had said. But Nyxobas had transformed the entire landscape. My former home, overtaken by these miserable creatures.

Come on, witches. Open that portal.

Thousands of pale eyes, running for us over the gnarled forest roots.

A blast of powerful magic rippled out over the earth, vibrating through my bones. I fell to the ground, and Ruadan screamed my name.

I pushed myself up from the earth, gripping my sword hard. When I rose, I caught a glimpse of the portal gleaming behind me. It glowed with the blue and gray of seas and storms, and lightning struck its surface.

The two witches jumped in, but Ruadan was waiting for me at the portal's edge, holding out his hand to me.

I charged for it as fast as I could, and when I reached it, I slammed into his body, knocking him into the portal with me.

We sank deep beneath the salty water.

CHAPTER 24

I climbed out of the portal and into Aenor's shop. The portal's opening was narrow, but it still filled most of the space. Aenor and Cora had already slipped behind the counter. Next to me, Ruadan hoisted himself out, seawater dripping off his muscled body.

Aenor turned and nailed the waterlogged demon heart to the wall.

Exhaustion had sapped my strength, but I now felt more frantic than ever to find my parents. Now I knew Baleros had gotten to them.

In the center of the room, the portal closed, and I steadied myself against the wall, still catching my breath. "What do we need to do now? You said we needed something for this tracking spell. Some kind of blood—what else?" I realized I was shouting, and I probably shouldn't be yelling at the people who were helping us, but my panic was starting to dissolve my patience.

"We've got most of it here," said Aenor.

"But we don't have everything," added Cora.

"We need a...." Aenor blushed, and her gaze flitted nervously to Ruadan. "A satyr's ... you know."

"What?" said Ruadan, irritated.

"His *manhood*," Aenor whispered.

"His penis?" I blurted, baffled.

Aenor's cheeks were now as bright as Cora's hair.

I held up my hands. "I'm sorry. You go by the name Flayer of Skins, Scourge of the Wicked. And you live in a shop with hearts nailed to the wall, one of which I just saw you carve out of a demon's chest. You're covered in blood, which you seem fine with. And you can't say the word 'penis?'"

"I was born in a different time," she said defensively.

I blew out a long breath. "Well, my bag of satyr dicks is fresh out, so does anyone have any ideas?" Again, I found myself yelling at the people helping me. Maybe my little death-angel stint in Eden had brought out my unpleasant side.

Cora rubbed her eyes. "I should probably add that we've literally never found a satyr penis. They don't give them up very easily. They have a thing about wanting to keep them attached."

"Can't imagine why," I said.

"I know where we can get one," said Ruadan.

The room fell silent, and I blinked at him. "I'm not sure I even want to know."

Ruadan frowned. "Is it a problem if it's attached to the satyr, or do we need it severed?"

"We just need it to stir with," said Aenor.

Cora's brow furrowed as she considered Ruadan's proposal. "I mean, I suppose he could just sort of ... stick it in the potion and give it a good stir." She gyrated her hips, then cleared her throat. "Please forget that I just made those hip movements."

Ruadan shrugged. "It will be easier to convince a satyr to lend us his penis if we don't have to remove it."

I clapped my hands together. "Good, okay. Where do we find a satyr?"

"The Carnival of Secrets," said Ruadan. "All we need is a coin from the ringmaster to gain entrance."

I gripped his arm. "I'm not even really understanding the words you're saying right now. Just tell me the rest when we get there. Let's get on this now." I nodded at Aenor. "You two —get the potion ready, and we'll bring you the dick."

* * *

THIS TIME, the portal opened into what looked like a darkened city park, and Ruadan led me to a forlorn-looking circus tent. The tattered fabric looked as if it had been here for a century, and it flapped in the wind. It was a tiny thing, and it looked completely abandoned.

"We'll find a satyr in there?" I whispered.

"I think so. I haven't seen him since the worlds closed. It looks … smaller now."

At this point, I knew better than to sheathe my sword going into any new dark place. There was a good chance I'd be killing at least one person in there, especially since we were covered in seawater and blood and looked terrifying.

Side by side, we moved closer to the tent. Ruadan lifted the canvas flap, and it yawned open into complete darkness. For a moment, I felt the dizzy sense of standing on the edge of a void—that the tiny, ragged exterior belied the vastness within here.

Then, a light sparked—a silver sphere from Ruadan that floated in the air. It illuminated a faded, checkered floor and a man who stood before us wearing a mask of a horse's head. And behind him, striped curtains—no, not curtains. As the light rose, I saw that it was an impossibly tall woman, her skirts blocking our way. Blond mermaid hair waved over her shoulders, and she smiled down at us.

As we walked closer, she lifted her skirts, allowing us to walk between her legs.

I cleared my throat, finding all of this a bit awkward, and I resisted the weird impulse to look up between her legs as we crossed between them into a long, dimly lit hall. The length of this hall didn't seem possible, given the size of the tent outside, and yet here we were, walking toward a gold-framed door at the far end. A glass case on a stand stood by the side of the door.

As we drew closer, the gold door swung open, and a small, white-eyed man stepped out wearing a top hat. Then, the door slammed closed behind him, and a golden lock slid shut with a loud click.

Ruadan looked at me. "Let me handle this." He turned to the man and said, "We bring love in exchange for coin."

The little man reached into his pocket and pulled out a gold coin. He tossed the coin high into the air, and Ruadan caught it.

Ruadan turned to the glass case. For the first time, I had a good view of it. Inside sat a red-lipped wooden doll with bulging eyes, dressed in a sailor costume. Ruadan slid the coin into a slot below the doll, and a mechanical whirring noise started ticking, the doll's body jerking around.

Then, its head snapped toward me, eyes locked on mine. The doll's wooden mouth opened and closed. "Liora." He broke into high-pitched, disconcerting laughter, tinged with the sound of cranking gears.

My gaze flicked to Ruadan. *This satyr penis better be worth it.*

The doll creaked and jerked, shifting position. Its wooden mouth opened and closed. "To enter here, you must answer this question." More high-pitched laughter. "Liora. How did Nyxobas prophesy this would all end?"

Ice slid through my blood. I'd hidden the truth from Ruadan—again, and I knew how much he hated that. Could I get off on a technicality?

"Badly."

The doll twitched. "What did he say?" he barked.

"You have to be more specific, Liora," Ruadan prompted. "It's the only way to open the lock."

Anger roiled in my chest. Cora's words—the ones about the gods always winning, always controlling everything—were starting to get to me. I hated nothing more than feeling powerless. I glanced at the golden lock on the door. Could I hack through it with my sword? With enough strength, could I just smash the thing?

Then, I swallowed hard. If Ruadan said it was the only way in, then it was the only way in. Gods knew he had enough strength of his own, so brute force wasn't gaining us entry.

I stole another quick glance at Ruadan, and I steadied my breath. I clutched the hilt of my sword. "He said that this all ends with Ruadan dying, but I think it's bollocks so I didn't bother passing it on."

"Lie!" said the doll. A peal of shrieking, mechanical laughter.

I hated this little wooden bastard. "It's what he said. You asked what he said, and I told you."

"But you know Nyxobas doesn't lie," said the doll. More earsplitting laughter.

Dread fluttered in my skull. Whatever else happened, I didn't want to live in a world that Ruadan wasn't in.

I smacked the glass. "I answered your question. Let us through."

The doll went still, jerking to a halt.

I glanced at the door, and the lock slid open. The little man shifted out of the way.

Ruadan's eyes had darkened, like they did whenever he sensed a threat, whenever his life was at risk. Despite my assurances about Nyxobas's prophecy being bollocks, Ruadan believed it. "Why did you lie to me again?"

"Because I don't want it to be true!" I hissed. "I don't want to live in a world that you're not in. You and I belong together. I am Death, but you give me life. Your loss would stop time and blacken the skies. Your death would be *my* apocalypse."

The mechanical doll groaned, emitting another cackle.

I pointed at it. "If you died, my soul would die, too, and I'd turn into that fucking thing. A creaking, empty, dead-eyed husk devoid of real life. Do you understand? So it won't happen, because it can't. I'm Death, and I say when the apocalypse happens. Fuck your grandpa. That's it. End of story. Now let's move on from that wooden weirdo, and have a normal, focused mission procuring a satyr cock, shall we?"

Ruadan was staring at me, so intently and deeply that I felt as if he were seeing into my very soul. His magic skimmed and snaked over my skin like a caress, and he reached up to cup my cheek.

His touch was painfully light. The gentleness of it was like a knife to my heart, because it felt like a goodbye. I didn't want this now. This felt like the end. *This* was why I hadn't told him.

Before I could say another word, the door groaned open. I pulled away from Ruadan, not accepting his goodbye, and I took a step into the doorway. Flashing, colored lights pulsed over a tent crowded with people and swaths of bright silks in scarlet and cobalt.

Truthfully, the biggest draw to my eye were all the breasts. In the crowded tent, the women were hardly dressed.

Many of them were in sequined corsets that exposed them from the nipples up. Others wore thigh-high stockings and the tiniest of knickers. Many of the men were shirtless, their muscled bodies oiled, mustaches waxed into curls.

Brightly colored lanterns hung from the top of a peaked circus tent, casting lurid lights over half-naked acrobats above us, and a tightrope walker who wore only a bowtie, high heels, and a feathered bustier. A luxurious white lion prowled around the edge of the circus, and a naked woman with long blond hair rode a horse like Lady Godiva.

I tried to keep my eyes off all the writhing bodies around us—the thrusting and groping and gyrating hips. It was less of a circus and more of an orgy designed by a Victorian pervert.

I narrowed my eyes. "What did you say you used to come here for?"

I already knew how he was going to respond—with something vague and evasive like. "I didn't say, actually." To my surprise, he met my gaze evenly and said, "I'm an incubus. I came here to feed off lust, so I could gain strength."

"Oh. Right." He made it all sound so reasonable when he put it that way.

His gaze slowly made its way down my body. As it did, I looked down at myself, shocked to see that my own clothing had transformed. My leather trousers had changed into a tiny skirt, short enough that I was pretty sure my bum was peeking out the back. Thigh-high fishnet stockings covered my legs, and a tiny striped top stretched over my breasts— enough, at least, to cover the nipples. My bra had disappeared entirely. I yanked the tube top up higher, readjusting it.

Most annoyingly, my sword had vanished. "What the hells?"

"The circus master is the satyr. This is his magic."

I looked up at Ruadan, whose clothing had changed into a cloak that covered his entire body. Only his pale violet eyes shone out from beneath his cowl. That gaze now swept over my body, lingering over my curves, my breasts, my hips, and I could feel his magic licking at my body.

He gripped me by the waist, his touch again agonizingly light.

"Not now," I whispered into his neck. "Save that for later. *After* we save the world."

After we save the world—and you are still alive because I won't let you die.

His quiet growl trembled over my exposed skin.

"Now, where do we find this satyr?" I asked.

Ruadan tore his eyes away from me and looked around the circus tent.

A woman in a sheer bra and knickers walked up behind him and stroked his back, brushing a kiss over his neck. She was gripping a bottle of whiskey. "Been a long time since I've seen you, fae prince," she giggled.

I arched an eyebrow at her. With her attention focused on Ruadan, I reached for the whiskey bottle in her hand. I might be needing this at some point. "Do you mind if I just…?"

She didn't notice as I pulled it from her grip.

Ruadan quirked a smile. "Celeste. Do you know where I can find Andre?"

"No time for me tonight?" She pouted.

"Not tonight, love," I said. "We need Andre. We need his penis, more precisely."

She let out a long sigh. "Don't we all?"

"Not like that— Never mind. Where is he?"

She pointed across the tent. "You'll find him there, watching the glitter wrestling."

We started weaving through all the lovers, the contortionists, and the wandering bears who were wearing more clothing than most of the women.

At last, we reached a particular ring. There, we found a golden satyr, standing proud. For a man with goat legs, he really wasn't bad-looking, his face model-perfect, hair golden and wavy. Curled horns swooped back from his head, and the fur on his legs was the same beautiful amber as his hair. I tried not to look at his enormous erection, though I was fully aware it would be coming into play later this evening.

Ruadan sped up his gait, and I tried to keep up with him.

As we approached, the satyr turned to us, arching his eyebrows in surprise. "Ruadan! It's been yonks!" Then, his expression darkened. "Wait a moment. I forgot you were with the Institute. You are, aren't you? Bloody fascists. Assassinating everyone. I was doing wonderful business in London before you forced us all into this closed world. I need fresh blood in here, you know?" He licked his lips, and he swept his gaze down my body. "Like this pretty little thing. Saucy minx you got here. Can I *have* her?"

I resisted the urge to tell him this saucy minx was death personified, though the idea of wilting his raging boner was appealing. Instead, I smiled, playing nice. We needed his help.

"I'm taking you back to London, Andre," said Ruadan. "You can recruit for fresh blood there until it's time to return to your world."

His eyes widened. "Why would you do me this favor?"

"We're going to need your penis," I said.

He smirked, purring, "Don't they all?"

"No, I mean we need it to save the world," I added.

"Of course you do." He put his hands on his hips, beaming. "I've been waiting for this moment all my life."

CHAPTER 25

The grim look on Aenor's face when we returned to her shop immediately told me something was wrong. As Ruadan helped Andre out of the portal, Aenor pulled me behind the counter, her nails digging into my skin.

"What's happening?" I hissed.

"I am here to save the world!" Andre proclaimed.

Aenor's dark eyes were on me alone. "Okay, good job on … *that*, but I have bad news."

"What?"

"One of my little sparrow spies was watching the Institute. And it seems that while you were fetching the satyr, Baleros came for your mist army. He destroyed them."

My stomach fell. "How is that possible?"

Ruadan cursed in Fae. "They're unprotected now."

Aenor shook her head, frowning. "He used powerful fire magic. He dissolved the mist army with flames. They're gone. Evaporated."

"This fucker has two gods working for him!" I shouted.

"This won't end well for him," Ruadan said again. But since I had no idea of the specifics on how that would backfire, it wasn't terribly comforting. "And we can get the mist army back, I think. Just not right now."

Cora stepped forward and tugged on my arm. "Let's get the spell done, at least. Once your father cures the knights, the Institute won't be quite as vulnerable."

I followed Cora, and we all crammed into Aenor's tiny, bone-decorated bedroom. Aenor stood against the wall, shielding her eyes as Ruadan directed Andre to the sea-green potion on the ground.

I did my best to not to watch Andre thrusting himself into the bubbling potion, and I was *definitely* pretending not to hear the unsettling sighing noises he was making. The news about the mist army had already nauseated me enough.

"Okay!" I shouted. "I think that's quite enough stirring, Andre. Am I right, Aenor?"

"I'm sure it's fine," she called out from under her hands.

"All right, Andre," said Ruadan in a weary tone that suggested he'd had to stage this kind of intervention before. "You have done the world an immeasurable service."

Andre rose, grinning from ear to ear. "My glorious priapism will be praised in hymns and ballads from now until the end of time."

I nodded. "That's right. Lots of ballads. Now move along. Go around the portal to get to the door, and say hi to Karen on your way out."

The floor creaked as he crossed out of the room.

Aenor's features brightened as soon as he was gone. "Okay. Good. Let's find your dad, shall we?" She crossed to the bubbling potion on the ground. "Cora, I'll need your help." Green magic sparked along her arm and charged down the end of her fingertips.

Cora stepped out of the corner of the room and summoned her own magic—a beautiful gray-blue that flickered around her hand. A phantom wind billowed through the room, lifting our hair, whipping at our skin. I had the strangest sensation of flying, that a salty tempest was buffeting us in this cramped room.

Their colored magic mingled above the potion, a stunning turquoise. My heart slammed hard against my ribs like a battle drum. At last, I'd find out where my parents were. I'd wrap my arms around my mum for the first time since I was a little girl.

The cloud of shimmering blue-green magic bloomed and pulsed above us. Then, an image began to take shape within the swirls of magic—stone arches, wood pews, stained glass windows—an ancient-looking church with a vaulted ceiling.

The vampire had said something about an old church. Baleros was in one, wasn't he?

"St. Bartholomew's," said Ruadan. "It's not far from here."

I stared at it, starting to believe it at last. I was about to find my parents.

Aenor dropped my mother's cherry-red hair into the cauldron next. The cloud of magic swirled a bit, then reformed to look like the same church. They were *both* there.

"They're together," I breathed.

But what the hells were they doing in that church?

They were in trouble, somehow. Baleros had trapped them. There was simply no other explanation.

I snatched my bag off the floor, now with a fresh stock of whiskey. "Let's go get my parents."

* * *

THE SUN WAS STARTING to rise by the time we neared Smithfield, tingeing the city with coral. Even after I'd left the circus world, I'd remained in this stupid tiny outfit, and I tugged up my little striped tube top to cover my nipples. We'd

165

borrowed swords from Aenor, but her clothes were too small for me.

Ruadan's gaze slid to me. "What do you expect to see when we find your father?"

"I have no idea. But I imagine we're...." I was about to say *rescuing him*, but then I felt stupid. He was the bloody Horseman of Death. He didn't need saving. "I don't know."

If he was okay, why hadn't he come to find me once Nyxobas had let him out of Eden? Finding his daughter should have been the first thing on his agenda. Adonis. Thanatos. Death himself. What in the heavens and hells would stop him from hunting his only child down at his first chance?

"Aenor said his curse had never taken hold," Ruadan added. "What if Baleros figured out how to reverse that?"

"You're being kind of a downer right now, Ruadan." I refused to give credence to this theory. "Let's cross that bridge when we come to it."

We moved swiftly along the narrow alleyways. No portals for us this time, since ripping a watery hole in the earth tended to attract a fair bit of attention.

Despite what Ruadan had said, I couldn't entertain the idea that my father's seal had been opened, unleashing his curse.

I breathed in Ruadan's smell: the apple and pine scent that had started to seem like home to me. As I did, I felt a fierce desire to protect him. And that meant acknowledging when threats might be real. My soul felt like it was ripped open as I imagined a deadly showdown between my father and my favorite demigod.

"I can't die from his death powers," I said quietly. "You can, if they're powerful enough."

My throat went dry at the thought of Ruadan growing sick with the Plague. Somewhere inside me, I had the power to stop this death magic, except that I had no idea how to control it.

I touched his arm. "Look, I have no idea what will happen. But you have your own way of gaining strength if you need it." I flashed him a sad smile. "All you have to do is tell me you don't ever want to see me again." All he had to do was break my heart.

The look he gave me pierced me to the core. He opened his mouth to reply, but before he could get a word out, a shadow crossed over us. Something above had blotted out the sun for just a moment.

My blood roared as I glanced up at the heavens.

My stomach clenched at the sight of two winged creatures swooping above us—dark angels, wings outstretched, one much larger than the other. No—demons, probably. Silhouetted against the rising sun, their features were obscure. My heart slammed like a war drum. They both had bows and quivers slung over their backs, and their aerial position was a huge advantage.

Here, in the sunlight, Ruadan and I wouldn't be able to move through the shadows the way we could at night.

I sucked in a sharp breath. "Can you see who that is?"

"Maddan." Ruadan squinted into the sunlight as they swooped overhead. "The smaller one is Maddan. The other … I don't know yet."

I didn't like the way they were swooping above the alley, like vultures eying up their prey.

Then, Maddan nocked an arrow, aiming it directly at us.

Bollocks.

I readied my sword, but when Maddan unleashed his arrow, Ruadan reached up, deflecting it with his sword.

"We're going to need to run, but they can hit us easily from their vantage point. We'll just have to go fast." The air frosted as Ruadan summoned a blast of shadow magic to hurl at our celestial attackers. Then he shouted something in Ancient Fae that I was pretty sure was a vile swear. "They're absorbing the shadow magic. Are you ready?"

"Wait." Running through an alley left us vulnerable, and we'd just get hammered from above. Tingles raced down my spine, and I could feel the death angel ready to erupt out of my body. Good. We actually needed her, now, to slaughter the demons above us. "Not yet, Ruadan," I said. "Cover me for a second. I have another idea."

Just had to make sure I didn't lose control completely.

Ruadan yanked me by the waist, pushing me against the wall just under a gutter overhang in the alley that shielded us a bit. I reached into my bug-out bag and yanked out the whiskey I'd taken from Celeste. I took a long, glorious sip. Then another.

Above, the larger demon started screeching in a high-pitched voice. I couldn't quite hear what he was saying, but there was something oddly familiar about it. How did I know that voice?

Ruadan pulled me tight against him, the arrows coming faster now. I could feel the air start to cool with his dark magic.

As I drank deeply from my bottle, Ruadan gaped at me. "We're waiting here just so you can drink whiskey?" he asked incredulously.

I drained the last drop. At last, I felt the comfortable buzz that I needed not to slaughter the whole world. "I need to drink whiskey so I can fly."

"What?" he barked. "You have to drink whiskey to fly? That's a shit superpower."

I'd had no idea that Ruadan used words like *superpower*. There were a lot of things I still had to learn about him, which meant we had to get out of here alive.

"I'll distract them from above, and you run away."

"I'm not taking part in a plan that involves the phrase 'you run away.'"

"Look, there are literally no good options here, so don't act like there's a better plan." I glanced at the mouth of the alley, and my pulse raced as I saw a flicker of movement. Demons were waiting for us to come out. When Ruadan got to the end, they'd trap him and cut the World Key right off his chest.

"Let's go," said Ruadan.

"Wait!" I grabbed his arm. "They're waiting for us at the other end. It's an ambush."

CHAPTER 26

The thought that there was still so much I didn't know about Ruadan occurred to me a second time. We had to get out of here so I could learn every single thing about him, about every moment of his long life.

Arrows were slamming into the wall next to us.

But right now, I had one crucial question. "Ruadan, can you fly?" I shouted. "Winged creatures can fly." *Thunk.* "Except chickens, penguins. Ostrich." *Shit, shit. Focus, Liora.* "My point is, now would be a good time to fly."

Thunk. Thunk. Arrows hit the wall on the other side of us, and we pressed into each other as tightly as possible.

"I can only fly when my incubus side comes out. And that only happens when I'm threatened."

"Are you fucking kidding me?" It came out like a screech, melding with the screeching of the demon above. The arrogance of a demigod. We were trapped in an alley, hammered with arrows by demons from above. On either side of the alley, more demons were waiting to kill us. But Ruadan didn't feel threatened. No, this was just an ordinary morning, apparently.

I'd only seen him transform twice. Once with me; the other time had been in the tunnels, when his old childhood tormentor—the serpentine Caoranach—had nearly killed him. She had been the one who *really* got to him.

I pulled him tight against me. "I'm sorry."

"For what?"

"For what's about to happen."

Then, I grabbed his throat as tight as I could, and I felt his body go rigid. I stood on my tiptoes, getting as close to his ear as I could.

I mimicked the lilting fae accent and deep voice of the Caoranach. "I've been here since before the angels," I said, in a voice that sounded exactly like hers. "Before the fae. I am one of the Old Gods. Your pain was finer sustenance than my tea."

Then, I bit his neck as hard as I could, drawing blood.

Black, leathery wings swooped down behind him, blocking out the sun above us. Star-flecked darkness swirled in his eyes and two dark horns gleamed on his head; a hand at my throat, black claws piercing my neck. For just a moment, I wondered if this was the worst idea I'd ever had, born from the whiskey I'd just chugged. Then, my breathing slowed again. My beautiful nightmare, a god dredged from primordial depths.

I might be death incarnate, but Ruadan still had the ability to send a shiver of primal fear up my spine. A voice in the ancient part of my brain told me to run, but I knew better. Even his monstrous side wouldn't hurt me.

"There you are," I said. "I love you. Even your ill-tempered side."

I'd never told him I loved him before. Now that it was out of my mouth, the terrible weight of those unspoken words had lifted off my chest. Now, I never wanted to stop saying it.

An arrow slammed against his wings, bouncing off—a

useful shield. Snarling, he pulled his hand away from my throat. Now, his gaze was sliding down my body, taking in the tube top that had slid down, one of my nipples peeking out. He growled quietly, then grabbed me by the waist, holding his sword in the other hand.

He'd gone from primal demigod of wrath to a lust monster. His magic stroked my skin like a dangerous caress. As arousal stirred in my own body, I could see him feeding from it, and his dark magic bloomed from his body.

Ruadan's wings had formed a shield around us, protecting us from the oncoming hail of arrows. Thin veins of silver shone in his wings, and light shone through the membranes. They looked thin, but they were protecting us.

I reached up to touch his black wing, and he sucked in a sharp breath, muscles tensing. His lust magic stroked over my bare skin, and his body glowed.

"Are your wings indestructible?" I asked.

His eyes had swept down to my breasts, and he cupped one of them, thumb stroking over my nipple. "Not quite. Nothing is indestructible."

My breasts peaked under the full, intense stare of an incubus.

And this was the problem with Incubus Ruadan. He might have wings, but his focus wasn't necessarily in the right place. Even with his powerful wings forming a dome around us, we couldn't stay here forever. The demons waiting for us at the mouths of the alley were about to trap us in here, and his wings wouldn't shield us for long.

Footfalls echoed off the alley walls, and Ruadan's head whipped to the right. The air turned to ice. The demons had decided to come for us.

"We need to get out of here," Ruadan snarled.

"I know. That's what I've been saying. Now. You need to use those big wings right now. And I need to use mine."

I will crush my enemies into the realm of the dead.

Ruadan grabbed me around the waist, and his powerful wings began thumping the air, lifting us out of the alley, into the coral morning sun rays. I gripped my sword in one hand and looped the other around his neck.

I will ensnare your bodies in chains of darkness.

A volley of arrows slammed into us, most of them hitting Ruadan's wings—but one of them pierced his leg.

I breathed in Ruadan's piney scent, then I whispered, "Let go."

My wings weren't out yet, and to my surprise, he trusted me enough to drop his grip on me anyway. For just a moment, I plummeted. My bug-out bag dropped to the ground, but I clung tightly to the sword.

I am the beginning and the end.

Then, dark euphoria spiraled through me as my own wings burst from my shoulder blades. Cool morning air whipped over my body. I'd been meant for the skies, and up here, I felt clear-headed.

I started flying in an erratic path, trying to make myself harder to hit. The pace of incoming arrows now suggested to me that they were running out. Ruadan's leather wings were carrying him toward Maddan, and I started to head for the other demon.

The sun blinded me, and it took a moment before I could focus on the second attacker—the larger one, whose screeching pierced my eardrums.

He was nocking another arrow. I finally recognized what he was saying.

"One, two, threeeeeeeee!"

"Barry?" The bloody caveman? Was there anyone Nyxobas hadn't transformed in the shadow hell?

Barry loosed his arrow, and I blocked it with my sword.

I enshroud your body with rot.

I angled my wings, flying faster for Barry. Up close, Barry looked quite a bit different than the hunched little Neanderthal I'd found in the dungeons. This Barry was enormous and muscled, his body covered in brown hair. His teeth were long and yellow, pointed at the ends, and pale eyes burned with hatred. Fresh out of arrows, he screeched and pulled a sword from his sheath.

Battle fury crackled up my spine as I reached him.

I swung for him, and he managed to deflect it. On the second slash, I sliced the quiver off his back, the tip of my blade carving into his skin.

"One, two, threeeeee!" A nasal screech, straight from the depths of hell.

Our blades clashed, sparking in the ruddy morning light. His stench was unbearable. Did showers not exist in the void? Whatever the case, Nyxobas had dutifully transformed him into a powerful warrior.

At this point, I wanted to slaughter Nyxobas myself.

Death has dominion over all gods.

For someone who looked like a winged caveman, Barry moved swiftly, his swordsmanship sophisticated. Our position had shifted, no longer over the little alley but in the skies above Smithfield. Centuries ago, these streets had run with the blood from butchered cows and executed traitors, or from victims burned by fanatical queens for heresy. Today, they'd run red with the blood of demons if I could help it.

"Barry lonely in the void!" he yelped.

His plaintive voice was worse than his attack, and the whining tone threw me off. Still, I was driving him back, controlling the fight and dominating him.

My gaze flicked back to Ruadan. To my horror, I realized he was no longer fighting Maddan alone—an entire horde of shadow demons had flocked to him. He moved in a blur, an explosion of dark, shadowy magic that froze the air. But there were so many of them, descending like a plague of locusts.

"Bollocks!" Barry had been acting as a distraction, pulling me away from Ruadan when I needed to keep him safe. Ruadan, of course, was the real target. I needed to act as his guard.

Now, several shadow demons were flying closer, still in the distance but moving for him. Had Baleros managed to transform each and every one of these demons in the void?

No, he probably hadn't needed to. All demons hated the Shadow Fae, since we tended to assassinate them. All Baleros had to do was get the word out across the earth to the demons hiding in the shadows, underground, afraid for their lives—an uprising was beginning: *The Great Rebellion starts in London. Live free; kill the Shadow Fae.*

It was a wonder the Institute had lasted as long as it already had.

I had to end this little skirmish now and get over to Ruadan.

CHAPTER 27

I positioned myself just above Barry's dark wings.

He opened his mouth. "One, two, threee—"

"Shut up, Barry!" I bellowed. I brought my sword down hard into his wings, carving through bone and muscle.

He yelped like an animal, then spiraled out of the skies, falling hard into Smithfield Square.

I glanced at Ruadan. The man was terrifying, a vortex of dark magic and icy air. Blood covered his body, but his sword hung at his waist. This savage version of Ruadan was ripping one of Maddan's wings off using his bare hands. No *wonder* Ruadan kept his brutal side under tight wraps.

Like a sadistic child toying with a fly, Ruadan ripped the second wing off Maddan. The bloodied, wingless creature began to fall to earth.

I swooped lower, racing for Maddan as he fell, nearly free-falling myself.

Death to the Prince of Elfhame. Death to Baleros's allies.

I swung. My blade sliced through his neck, carving his head from his body.

I shot Ruadan an irritated glare, as if to say *that's how you*

176

kill, a perfectly civilized decapitation the way the gods and nature intended, but he completely missed the look because another winged demon was moving closer now. And at any moment, more would be upon us.

My wings thumped the air. The thrill of destroying Maddan was short-lived—a high-pitched scream turned my head.

"One, two, *threeeeeeee!*"

Barry's bloody wing had *already* healed, and he flew for me again—this time clutching sharpened iron stakes. Demon Barry was a lot sturdier than Maddan. And where the hells had he got the iron stakes from?

He hurled one at me. But just before it reached me, I snatched it in midair. The iron burned my palm, but I twirled it around and hurled it at Barry, catching him in the wing.

Death to the allies of Baleros.

The iron spike ripped his wing a second time.

"Threeeeeeeeeee!" he shrieked. He tumbled to the pavement, blood streaming from his body.

I'd finish him off for good later. Right now, I needed to help protect Ruadan from the legions of shadow demons surrounding him. We were drastically outnumbered, and cold rage spurred me on faster, the wind whipping over me as I flew closer to Ruadan.

Of course Baleros waited until the sun rose to stage his real attack. In the light, we couldn't leap away.

I'll be a blight on the earth.

I longed to just unleash my death magic, but if it was powerful enough, I'd take Ruadan down with it and finish the knights for certain. Instead, I joined the fray. My sword was a tornado of steel, hacking into wings, carving off horns and limbs. Ruadan moved swiftly and gracefully, like a night storm. *Strike, thrust, hack.*

The blood of our enemies rained over Smithfield.

Demons, their wings decimated, plummeted to the pavement.

Protect the one I love.

I fought with the fierceness of a king protecting his fortress, every inch of me now moving precisely.

But more demons kept coming, some of them flying behind me. I couldn't whirl fast enough to take them all on.

From behind, a sword cut into my wings.

I'd been stabbed many times, cut with swords and knives. A fire demon had singed my entire left leg once. But I'd never experienced the exquisite pain of a wing injury, an agony that seemed to rip me apart from the inside out. It spread through my body and set up camp inside my skull.

Then, the swoosh of air around me as I fell.

I slammed down hard on the concrete, body cracking with the fall. Was I screaming? Pretty sure I was.

From my cleaved wing, sharp pain ripped through me. I rolled onto my hands and knees. I'd lost my sword in the fall, and I desperately scanned the pavement for it.

"One, two, *threeeeeeeeeee!*" My head whipped to the side to see if Barry was coming for me. He wasn't. Instead, he was gripping iron spikes and slamming them into the ground with a disturbing sort of glee. His wings may have been ripped, but he didn't seem to mind, so intent was he on stabbing the pavement with iron spikes. What was he doing? He was obviously completely mental now, but his physical strength was truly stunning.

I had no time to contemplate that further, because another demon was moving for me, his body a vortex of darkness with two burning white eyes. His form flickered in and out, but I got glimpses of a lithe, leathery demon with long claws.

Shit. He moved like the Wraith, and I'd lost my weapon.

I pushed myself to my feet, wishing my wings would

retract like they normally did. Apparently, that didn't happen when one of them had been ripped.

As the leathery demon reached me, I burst into action using only my body. I hammered his desiccated face with my fist, and I kicked him hard in the chest. He was moving just as fast, but I managed to dominate, landing one punch after another.

A primal instinct in the back of my mind, an invisible thread that connected me to Ruadan alerted me that something was wrong. I glanced up at the skies. My heart stuttered at the sight of Ruadan careening for the earth, his wings ripped, bleeding.

"No," I whispered.

It was just enough of a distraction that I lost the advantage. In the next moment, the demon's clawed fingers were around my throat, piercing my neck.

Baleros's second law of power: Caring for others makes you weak.

I kicked him hard in the crotch, and he dropped his grip on me. My victory was short-lived. Already, another creature was ripping at my wings from behind. Pain screamed through my body.

I was surrounded, but my survival instincts were still keeping me focused. I kicked a demon so hard in the throat that he dropped his sword, and I snatched it as it fell. I swung it in wild arcs, trying to keep the demons at bay. I had to kill them all to get to Ruadan.

Where the hells was Baleros? I could almost feel his corrupted presence tainting the air.

I swung at the demons around me. Then, an iron arrow from above pierced my chest. I fell back onto the pavement.

Pinned to the ground by half a dozen demon hands, my wings and spine splintered with pain. Someone kicked the sword away from me. I bucked and thrashed, trying to break free.

Panic stole my breath as I spied a glimpse of Ruadan on the other side of Smithfield. I caught just a fleeting instant, but it was enough to know what was happening. Enough to rob my mind of all sense for one horrible, quiet moment.

The demons had surrounded him, and they were driving iron spikes into the ground through his wings.

My world tilted.

They wanted to pin him there like a butterfly, then carve the World Key off his chest.

He could have made a portal to get out of here. Why the hells hadn't he made a portal to escape?

I searched for a shadow I could leap to, but in the bright morning light, they were few and far between, and the demons kept hitting me. I growled, fighting wildly against the demons gripping my arms.

That's when a thought struck me with the sharpness of an arrow to my skull. Ruadan was staying because of *me*. He'd promised to stay by my side and to keep me safe. He'd promised he wouldn't run away. And he wasn't breaking that promise now. Even if he *really* should be.

A blow to the side of my head dizzied me for a moment. My death magic threatened to burst out of me.

If it weren't for me, Ruadan would be out of here by now.

And if it weren't for Ruadan, I'd probably be spilling my death magic into every living creature around me right now. I'd kill all of London in one glorious death spasm and free myself from the attackers beating the living shite out of me.

Instead, I was grappling here with a demon horde.

Caring for others makes you weak.

Ruadan needed strength, and I needed a real weapon again.

A demon kicked me in the head, and I fell forward. Where was that sword?

Focus, Liora. Get to Ruadan.

I ripped a loose cobble from the ground—a possible weapon. I started to stand, ready to kill with it. But before I could use it, another arrow pierced me from behind, and I fell to my knees again. Where had that sword gone?

Get up, Liora. Get to Ruadan before someone robs the world of the fae prince—the boy who made his mother a crown of flowers, who grew up to be a warrior.

The world needed him, and so did I.

I rose again, fury igniting me with a pure clarity, and my gaze locked on my newest attacker—a winged demon with enormous fangs. The cobble was out of my hand in a fraction of a heartbeat, and it slammed into his skull, cracking it. I snatched his sword from him before he hit the ground.

My desperation to get to Ruadan burned the fear from my body. There was nothing now except my sword and the wounds of my enemies.

Snarling like a savage thing, I hacked my way out of the crowd of attackers, running for Ruadan. I needed to tell him to open the portal—*could* he open the portal with that iron pulsing through his blood?

Probably not.

And I was no longer strong enough to get him out of here unless I went full angel.

CHAPTER 28

I ran for him anyway, sprinting across the square, but I was still in the stupid satyr heels. I shadow-leapt to a shady tree not far from him—but there was just so much godsdamned light around. It must have been magically created.

From behind, a demon grabbed at my hair and my wings, slowing me down. I whirled, swinging my sword to sever the creature's body in two.

When I turned back to face Ruadan, panic slammed into me. A cloaked figure stood above him, knife glinting. Bright magic lights blazed above him, eliminating shadows. I couldn't leap any further.

Even with the cloak, I knew it was Baleros. I broke into a run again, my mind screaming. *Stop him.* Baleros brought the knife up above Ruadan, ready to skin him.

A furious roar from Ruadan shook the stones beneath my feet. My spirit leapt as Ruadan ripped himself free from his iron pinions, tearing at his wings. The pain must have been unbearable, shredding his leathery wings. Ruadan caught

Baleros's hand before the knife could plunge into his chest. Then, Ruadan twisted his arm, breaking it.

I was almost at him now, my sword ready. Baleros's dark eyes shifted to me. For the first time, I knew he was afraid of me.

I drove the blade into his neck, severing his spine and throat in an instant. His body burst into flames, knocking me back with the heat. I coughed as the scent of charred flesh filled the air.

A temporary victory—nothing more. The fire goddess had claimed his body. Ash wafted into the air around us. He could come back at any moment, revived by the goddess he served. And worse, the demons were still surrounding us, intent on our deaths.

Ruadan wrapped his arms around my waist. His leather wings were forming a barrier once more, but they wouldn't last forever. The rips in his wings made my chest tight.

"They're after me," he whispered into my ear. He lifted one of his arms over my shoulders and carefully cupped my head in the cocoon of his wings. "They're after the World Key, not you. I can cover you while you get out of here."

"I'm not leaving you here, you moron," I whispered back. "Make a portal."

"I can't. There's too much iron in my blood." He loosened his hold on me. "When I open my wings—"

I locked my arms tightly around him. I wasn't letting him go. I wasn't letting Baleros get his hands on the Prince of Emain again.

"Fine," I said. "Open your wings."

Light poured in as Ruadan's wings parted, but I kept my grip tight on his waist, squeezing him to my body.

I am the alpha and the omega.

With an iron will, my broken wings lifted us into the air

with all the strength I had left. "Hold on to me," I said as we rose above Smithfield.

He weighed roughly as much as a truck, and pain screamed through my shoulder blades. He gripped onto me, too, holding me tightly around the waist with his powerful arms. His wings were beating the air slowly, but they'd been damaged more than mine. I didn't think he could fly on his own.

"What the hells are you doing?" he said. "I told you to run."

"Was that an order?"

"*Yes.* I'm the Grand Master. Have you forgotten?"

"Almost there." I grunted with the effort. My grip on him was ferocious. Only a few feet to the churchyard.

My father was supposed to be in that church. Would we find him there?

I was barely holding on, unable to think clearly.

Two arrows *thunked* off Ruadan's wings. He snarled, tightening his grip on me.

We finally reached the gated churchyard, and I tried to move slower for a gentle landing, but my strength was giving out.

Good enough.

I let go of Ruadan, and he jumped to the ground, landing hard on a raised patch of grass between tombstones. I landed just after him, the impact shooting up my calves and thighs.

I searched the church for signs of my dad, but I didn't see him. I could *smell* him, the dark scent of myrrh. A sheen of shadow magic glimmered over the church, protecting it like a shield.

A loud *thud* from behind me turned my head. Already, a demon with an axe was trying to hack through the wooden door at the gate.

I ran for the ancient church doors, but as I touched the

metal doorknob, a blast of electric shadow magic knocked me back. I just barely managed to stop myself from falling back flat onto my broken wings.

"Dad?" I shouted at the church, like an idiot.

The church did not respond.

To our left, a demon with an arrow was aiming it over the iron gate. There really wasn't much cover here, and we needed a portal immediately. In the church's ancient, arched doorway, Ruadan began shielding me again with his wings. His powerful body pressed against mine, wings splayed open to keep me safe.

I turned to him. "You need to heal," I said, hoping the ferocity in my voice would convey my meaning.

If he wanted to gain strength, all he needed to do was tell me he didn't love me. He just had to say he never wanted to see me again. The power of that heartbreak would feed him with the strength of a thousand armies.

You're a monster, Liora, and you never should have been let out of your cage. That's what he needed to say to me—the truth that I carried with me at all times. That was all. The pain of a perfect betrayal would feed his broken body, and he could open a portal.

Instead, he was cupping my face.

"Do it," I whispered.

I couldn't entirely spell it out. If I said, *"Tell me you don't love me,"* and he repeated it like a puppet, I wouldn't believe his words. My heart wouldn't break enough. He had to crush my spirit in his own words. Why did he not get this?

"I love you," I prompted him. *Don't you get it? Feed, fomoire.*

He pulled me against his powerful chest, kissing my neck. "I love you, too," he murmured. "That's why we will keep each other safe."

Warmth spread through my belly. "You idiot. If you broke my heart, we could be getting out of here right now."

His dark, fierce gaze bored into me, then stroked down my body. He slid his hands down to my waist, gripping me possessively. "That's not the only way I grow strong." Dark seduction laced his voice.

Could I really give him the strength he needed right here, with the demons closing in on us?

I supposed lust wasn't the *worst* idea.

I pressed myself against him, standing on my tiptoes to kiss him. From my waist, his hands slid lower, cupping my bum under my barely existent skirt. He was teasing me just enough to make my blood roar.

For a fraction of a moment, I prayed to the gods that my dad wasn't in the church right now. Then, I forgot about him entirely, my attention completely focused on Ruadan's hands on my body and the silky feel of his tongue against mine. I hoisted myself up, wrapping my legs around his waist.

Ruadan pulled away from the kiss, then whispered in my ear, "Get ready for this."

That was all the warning I had before the ground opened up in the stone beneath us and I plunged into the cold waters. As the portal churned around me, I thought my wings would rip right off my back.

CHAPTER 29

Gasping for breath, I lay flat on my stomach on a bed of the softest moss I'd ever felt. The air smelled heavy and damp with honeysuckle and ferns. A river burbled nearby. Morning sunlight streamed through towering oaks, flecking the emerald earth with chinks of amber.

I inhaled again, catching the faint scent of apples on the breeze. So Ruadan had taken me back to his childhood home once more—back to Emain. This was home to him, the first place in his mind he'd imagine when he thought of safety.

Gods, I wanted to stay here with him forever, just living in the forest. Clean water, meals of mushrooms and honey, fish from the river. Just basically eating and sleeping and kissing Ruadan whenever I wanted.

Except that would mean leaving the Institute and possibly most of London to die a horrible death.

I felt as if every bone in my wings had been broken and poorly sealed back together again with duct tape. Turned out that wings were *fabulous,* and they could make you feel euphoric. They made you feel like a god. But the flip side was

187

that they made you vulnerable and could leave you a crumpled and broken heap on a forest floor.

"Wings are like love," I muttered into the moss.

"What?" Ruadan asked.

"Nothing."

I turned my head to look at him. Shirtless, he was crouching, pulling up clumps of moss from the earth. What was he doing? And more importantly, how was he moving? I supposed he'd probably been managing the pain of wing injuries for centuries, while this was a whole new world to me.

"What are you doing with the moss?" I asked.

"I need to fix your wings," he said. "You won't be able to transform to your normal form while they're broken like that."

"What about yours?" I asked.

"We'll heal my wings after."

My cheeks heated as I thought of what sort of healing that would entail.

He shifted closer to me. "This might hurt a bit at first," he said.

I held my breath, and I winced at the feeling of pressure on my right wing, but the moss was cool against it.

"This isn't ordinary moss," Ruadan murmured. "It's enchanted, from the Emain forest. With this and my magic, you'll heal fast."

Along with the moss, his magic slid over my wings, soothing all the pain. I breathed in and out deeply, taking in the rich forest air. Already, I could feel my wings growing stronger. Healing magic spiraled over my feathers, stroking each one, straightening their quills and down.

It occurred to me that Ruadan was perfectly savage and perfectly serene at the same time. He was a beast, comfortable with himself. And when I was with him, my mind felt tranquil. He excited my body with a wild intensity, and yet he was the only one who could calm the raging waters of my mind. He was the only one who could subdue Baleros's voice. My old master lived in the darkest hollows of my skull, whispering *monster*, and Ruadan was there to silence him.

Ruadan—god of sleep—had the power to make me feel normal and whole. And that was amazing magic indeed.

His fingertips brushed down my wings, stroking my delicate feathers, and I shivered at his touch. The tips of my feathers were immensely sensitive, and at that moment, I knew I never wanted anyone but Ruadan to touch them. I trusted no one like I trusted him.

His magic whispered over them, a healing balm that felt like it was made for me. I breathed in the charged, enchanted air of the Emain forest.

At last, when my wings felt completely strong once more, they retracted into my shoulder blades. I sighed and rolled over onto my back.

My little top had slid down somewhat, and bits of moss and soil stuck to the top of my breasts. I brushed them off, wondering precisely how many demons I'd exposed myself to when I'd been fighting in the ridiculous satyr-inspired outfit. Then, I pushed myself up to my feet.

Despite the gentleness of Ruadan's healing, I still had a monster before me. This was Ruadan the Incubus, not Ruadan the sophisticated Grand Master.

His dark gaze was as bestial and ferocious as ever. He looked *hungry* for me, his intensity charging the air around us. In the underground river, when I'd taken off my clothes in front of him, I'd been unable to meet his gaze—certain that if I had, the world would combust around us. Now, I could feel his eyes on me, and I wanted to burn in that inferno.

"Now you," I said.

With a sly smile, I tugged down my tube top until my breasts popped out, and I slid the top all the way down over my belly and hips, the curve of my arse, until I stepped out of it completely.

When I stood up again, Ruadan stared as my nipples hardened in the forest air. Goosebumps rose on my skin with the anticipation of his touch, and a pale flush spread over my chest.

Arching an eyebrow, I backed up against the rough bark of an oak. The feel of his silky magic on me was a sexual promise that made my toes curl, and I tugged up the hem of my short skirt.

His body had gone completely rigid, and a feral growl rumbled out of his chest. His wild magic skittered along my breasts and belly, and it stroked my thighs. We hadn't even touched yet, but he was looking at me like he wanted to devour me, and already, a molten hot ache was building between my legs. I wanted to feel his hands there, his tongue thrusting.

He made a low and bestial sound, and he started to move for me. I held up one finger, signaling for him to stop right where he was. Violet magic flared out from his body. He looked as if he were ready to rip this forest apart to get to me.

He'd get to me soon enough, but stoking desire was all about *just* the right amount of denial.

And right now, Ruadan's body was already responding to my desire. His muscles beamed with violet light as he fed off my lust, and his body was taut with anticipation. By the tightly coiled look of his muscles, he was using every inch of his restraint not to attack me right now. He took a step closer even though I'd told him not to, eyes coal-black. A muscle twitched in his jaw.

With his gaze penetrating me, I reached under my skirt,

hooking my thumbs into the hem of my tiny knickers, and I pulled those off, too, down to my ankles. The breeze—along with Ruadan's magic—kissed my bare thighs. Despite its coolness, my skin was hot. A strand of my lavender hair stuck to my cheek.

I left the tiny skirt on, but nothing else. Already, I was so turned on I couldn't think straight. I beckoned Ruadan closer, wildly aching for him. My thighs clenched as he took a step closer, and liquid heat arced through me.

Snarling, he moved for me like a beast let out of his cage. He gripped my wrists, pinning them over my head. My pulse pounded hard and fast, and my breathing sped up. My nipples brushed against his chest painfully lightly. His other hand was on my hip, his grip fierce.

I'd made him wait, and now he was in complete control. He kissed me slowly, savoring it.

I groaned, trying to move against him. Gods, I needed him now. I pulled away from the kiss for a moment, catching my breath, and I pulled my wrists from his grasp. I unbuttoned his trousers, staring into his dark eyes as I did. He gasped as my fingertips brushed against him.

"Tell me how you feel about me." The ultimate aphrodisiac.

With his free hand, he caressed my face. "You're perfect for me, as if the gods made us for each other. Even if you're flawed, the whole of you is perfect. If I lost you, I'd never sleep again." Now, his hand stroked down my body, palming one of my breasts. "Enough talking."

His mouth was hot on my neck, tongue flicking over my skin. At the apex of my thighs, a fiery, slick ache built so intensely I wanted to groan. Lust pounded through my blood, pulsing hot. One of his fingers stroked me, and I almost lost my mind. I'd made him wait before, and now I was on the verge of begging him.

"Ruadan." His name came out like a moan, pleading. I reached up for his wing, brushing my fingertip over the top. His body stiffened, fingers tightening on my arse.

I hooked my leg around one of his, and I ran my foot up the back of his leg, my little skirt riding up even higher. His gaze swept down between my thighs.

At that, he reached down and ripped the little skirt off me. My desire was almost unbearable as he lowered me to the ground, deftly managing to cup the back of my head. He was still being too gentle, too careful with me, the ache in my core demanding that he move faster.

I let my legs fall open, and he moved between them. I gripped him hard around his back, pulling him into me.

He slid into me, and I moaned his name. Our bodies merged as he filled me deeply. Everything left my mind except the feel of his slow, powerful stroke. He claimed my mouth with his, kissing me deeply as he thrust into me. My legs wrapped around him, and I thrust my fingers into his hair, trying to pull him closer as my hips moved against him.

It was like we'd been made for each other—my lover, perfect in his flaws, the one who made me feel safe and calmed the wild waters of my mind. We melded with each other, intertwined like flower stems in a wreath—no end and no beginning between us.

"I love you," I breathed into his neck.

As he whispered it back, ecstatic release rippled through my body, and I shuddered around him.

CHAPTER 30

*S*till naked, I curled around Ruadan's body on the soft, mossy earth. Completely satiated, he glowed with powerful shadow magic. He'd healed completely, and his wings, no longer broken, slid back into his body.

He stroked his hand down my back slowly. We couldn't stay here much longer. The Shadow Fae needed Adonis's power, and we had to return to London. But I needed just another moment here with him before we took on our enemies.

"Why this particular part of the forest?" I asked into his chest. "You were in immense pain. You nearly died. And in your panic, you took us to this particular part of Emain. Why here?"

He stroked my hair. "This is where I used to play as a very young boy. Before I joined the Shadow Fae and before Baleros trained me. Before I laid eyes on the Caoranach. I used to play here with my half-brothers."

I sucked in a sharp breath. His brothers had died when I'd unleashed my magic. "What were their names?"

"Mochan and Nuallan. Both were older than me. They

hunted boar here. They were brilliant hunters. We'd roast the meat over a fire at the end of the hunt. They let me drink their beer sometimes."

I smiled at his memories. Then, I lifted my head from his chest. "There are boar here?"

Ruadan kissed my neck. "They only come out at night. I carved my own spear from a branch. I didn't kill a single boar. I just liked being with Mochan and Nuallan. Before Baleros trained me, I wasn't suited to killing. I didn't like seeing the boars hurt. Obviously, I got better at it."

"Let's not talk about Baleros."

His hand stilled on the back of my hair. "But we do have to go capture him now."

I groaned. "I know. We need a plan," I said, willing my mind to clear from the haze of pleasure.

"We return to London. We find your father to heal the Shadow Fae, and we imprison Baleros in the Tower."

I cupped his face in my hands and stared directly into his eyes. "And then after we kill Baleros, you will give me a crown of wildflowers, and I will marry you."

Silence fell. For a moment, my heart stuttered, unsure of how he would respond. Then, an expression I'd never seen on Ruadan's face before—a completely unguarded smile. "Where I come from, females don't propose marriages."

"Pretty sure that's everywhere."

"But it's fitting that you would ask me. And how could I refuse?"

Smiling, I shrugged. "I mean, I wasn't even really asking, I was just telling you what's going to happen. And I'm death incarnate. So you really *can't* refuse."

His hand stroked down my back, and he leaned in for another kiss.

I felt as if the mossy earth were reaching up to keep me here with soft forest hands. Was this place enchanted, or was I overcome by the seductive magic of being with Ruadan?

In either case, Ruadan broke the spell by pulling away. "We have to get back to London."

I knew what he meant without him spelling it out. By this point, the Shadow Fae could be dead.

I sighed and sat up, frustrated to find that my only viable piece of clothing had been ripped in two. "I don't suppose there are any stray nymphs around here we could steal clothing from? I'd rather not reunite with my long-lost family with my fanny on display."

He rose. "So particular. I may have to rethink our marriage plans if you're that high-maintenance about everything."

The smile on his lips stopped me from throwing a clump of moss at him.

"I'll be back in a minute with some clothes for you," he said. "And while I'm off, we need to figure out how to discreetly approach the church. We know that the demons are waiting for us there. As soon as we return, they'll try to rip us apart again. If we portal in, they could be waiting for us with swords before we even breach the surface. We need to enter discreetly. Then, we have to get past the shadow demons and break through the bonds of shadow magic to get to your father without anyone knowing, in the broad daylight."

"You make it sound hard or something." I stood, slipping into my underwear. I'd wear a stolen dress, but stolen knickers were a bridge too far.

I closed my eyes, envisioning the layout of Smithfield Square. Any portal we opened nearby would be an obvious red flag. We might as well arrive with flashing lights, screaming *Hey demons! Come rip our wings off again! Fresh World Key skin for you!*

Unless there were something else for them to focus on….

I bit my lip. In the daylight, everything was a million times harder. There were a few shadows cast by the buildings and trees, but we'd have to be fast as lightning if we wanted to go undetected. I'd had a hard time finding the shadows in the chaos earlier. That meant knowing exactly where to jump ahead of time, with no time for scanning the horizon.

I chewed my lip, trying to visualize Smithfield Square. I was pretty sure there was concrete on one side, like a building of some kind….

The crunching of leaves pulled me away from my thoughts, and I looked up to find Ruadan crossing toward me with a black dress in his hand.

"You didn't have to kill anyone, did you?" I stood, pulling it from his hand.

"No," he shrugged, still glowing wildly. "I'm an incubus. It's not that hard to charm a dress off a nymph."

I glared at him.

"What?" he said. "I got you the dress you asked for."

"Fine." I pulled it over my head. "I had some thoughts about our plan. We need to create a distraction while one of us shadow-leaps over to the doors undetected and breaks through the shadow magic."

He scrubbed a hand over his mouth. "That's what I was thinking. I'll draw their attention toward me, and I can teach you how to break the bonds of shadow magic."

I crossed my arms. "How can you be the distraction? You're the one they want. They'll just surround you and Neanderthal Barry will rip you to shreds with iron spikes again."

"*Again?* That never happened."

"It nearly happened. The point stands. You're the target. They'll come right for you."

He shook his head. "I won't look like me."

"How? Neither of us have powers of glamour."

"With enough concentration and my newly recharged magic, there's one form I can take. At least for a few minutes, long enough to create a distraction that will terrify all of them."

I frowned. "What would terrify Baleros? He can't die. He just keeps coming back like a plague of locusts."

"With enough power, I can take on the form of my grandfather. Baleros won't know why Nyxobas has arrived, but a god showing up on your doorstep is never a welcome sight. No one tries to kill a god. You just have to move quickly, because I won't be able to hold his form forever."

"Okay. So we open up a portal at a safe distance, probably in a nearby building where they can't see us. You come out into Smithfield Square, you do your terrifying god thing. Meanwhile, I shadow-leap toward the church as fast as I can, and hopefully no one is looking at me because they're all focused on the terrifying god of the void."

"You have the lumen stone, so you'll be able to whisk through completely undetected. You have the shadow route mapped out in your mind, right?" he asked. "Because you won't have time to pause and scan for them."

I blinked. "Shadow route?"

"Where all the shadows would be falling at the time we arrive."

"I ... was there a tree?"

He stared at me, probably trying to ascertain if I was joking.

"I know there was a building of some kind," I added. "Probably several. Look, I was in the middle of being beaten to death by demons, so I failed to stand around memorizing shadow placements for possible future use. My mistake."

"Okay. We'll work on that. I'll open a portal into a building on Cock Lane."

I smirked at that, then hoped Ruadan hadn't seen the twitch of my lips. A thousand-year-old fae prince probably didn't titter at the word "cock."

"Do you know the Golden Boy of Pye Corner?"

I opened one of my eyes. "Is this a nursery rhyme?"

"There's a statue on the corner of that building—a chubby little boy made of gold that the humans stuck there because they foolishly believed the great fire of 1666 was a punishment for gluttony and not the result of one of Emerazel's temper tantrums. Close your eyes."

I did as he said. He touched my temple, and the image of the golden boy statue blazed in my mind. Now, I could remember seeing it. I could picture the whole street corner— the brick and stone and the fat golden statue. "Okay. I've got it now."

"We'll open the door of that corner building, below the statue. The sun will be casting shadows on the left side of Giltspur Street. From there, you'll shadow-leap toward the square."

With his hand on my temple, he talked me through each shadow—each tree, every dark corner beside the ancient hospital, and the shadows cast by the tombs in the churchyard.

Now, I had a clear shadow route in my mind, and I'd be able to traverse it almost instantly.

I opened my eyes. "And once I get to the church door? How do I break through the shadow magic?"

"You need to use the power of a god and meld with the magic."

"Good. Okay. How do I use the power of a god?"

He slid a silver ring off his pinky and slipped it onto my finger. As soon as he did, his magic spilled into me. I shivered at the intimate feel of a god's power in my body.

"My magic is imbued in this ring. Freshly charged, linked

to Nyxobas. He's the one who created the barrier on the church. I could feel it. When you get to the shield, you have to meld with the magic there. You'll slip into the void for just a moment as you do. Make sure you stay grounded. Focus on your feet."

"On my feet?"

He nodded. "Focus on their connection to the ground. It will keep you in our world. It should only take a moment. A fraction of an instant. Envision the barrier breaking apart."

Even with Ruadan's soothing magic billowing around me and racing through my body, my shoulders were growing tenser. Everything hinged on what happened after we opened that door into Smithfield.

Everything.

And the truth was, I had no idea what I'd find once I opened those church doors. I'd been imagining throwing the doors open to find my father locked in a cage. I imagined that he needed us to simply free him, and he'd burst forth from the church and save us all.

But who the hells knew what we were really up against? What if it was more than Nyxobas's magic trapping Adonis in the church? Gruesome, disturbing possibilities were spiraling through my mind.

Ruadan brushed a strand of my lavender hair out of my eyes. "What are you thinking, love?"

That we've been pursuing my dad this whole time, and what if he's not the answer we've been hoping for?

I filled my lungs with the forest air. "That I will rip the throat out of anyone who tries to hurt you. Anyone." I blew out a long breath. "Also, that I've sobered up, and I'm all out of whiskey."

"You don't need it."

"Except, without it, I might kill everyone if I have to let the death angel out."

"You won't."

"That's sweet." I pulled him toward me in a hug, and I murmured into his chest, "But you just think that because you're blinded by love." I twisted his magic-imbued ring around my thumb. "Since you agreed to marry me, I'll just consider this our engagement ring."

He leaned down and picked a dandelion from behind me. "No, I'll make one."

"A wreath of wildflowers. Of course." I plucked it from his hand, then twirled the dandelion stem between my fingertips. I brushed the soft yellow tip against his nose. "Give it to me once we've chained Baleros in iron."

CHAPTER 31

*D*ripping with icy portal water, we stood in an old stone building at one of the corners near Smithfield. The gods' magic from the ring electrified me.

Ruadan looked back at me. "I'm going to cloak myself in the form of the night god now. In his true form, Nyxobas has a dizzying effect on people. Like vertigo. You might want to avert your eyes. I'll stride into the square, and then you need to leap into the shadow route directly after me. Do you remember it?"

"Yes. I remember it exactly."

"Good. Look away as I transform."

I stared at the floor as the temperature plummeted in the room, and tendrils of shimmering dark magic snaked in whorls and eddies around us. He'd told me not to look, but I stole a quick glance at the form before me—a black cloak, perfect features pale as moonlight, hair coal-black, eyes gleaming with silver. Shivers rippled over my body, and I was overcome by a disturbing sense of trespassing. The real face of Nyxobas was something I was never meant to see.

Looking directly at him was a violation of a kind—and a strangely addictive one.

Ruadan was right—I did feel as if I were standing at the edge of a cliff, and that I wanted to throw myself over the edge, to lose myself in a vast nothingness. I forced myself to tear my eyes away from him, and he swept out the door.

Now, Liora.

It was time. Everything hinged on the next few minutes, and my pulse raced out of control.

I resisted the urge to stare at Nyxobas's strange, star-cloaked beauty again, and I stared at the shadow across the street—my target.

My pulse roared in my ears. Cold shadow magic whispered through my blood, made more powerful by the ring Ruadan had given me. I mentally melded with the shadow by the old hospital walls, and I leapt.

From there, I was already on to my next target—a shadow beside a tree within the square—then the next—the darkness at the exact spot where the Scottish rebel William Wallace had been eviscerated nearly a thousand years ago. I refused to let myself look at Ruadan, but I was vaguely aware that shadow demons were *literally* crawling from their hiding spots, prostrating themselves before their god.

With the demons' attention occupied, I leapt to the gate before the church, peering through the hole to the church-yard. Then, my final leap—to the shadows in the arched doorway of the ancient church. My heart was a wild beast as I made the final leap to the church door, where shadow magic glistened in dark waves. I stepped into the barrier, melding with it—just as Ruadan had told me to.

And just as he'd said, vertigo dizzied me. For a moment, I felt myself plummeting into the depths of the void.

Questions spiraled in my mind. Was I really here at all, a superhero with a stunningly hot lover? A girl who thought she was destined to save the world? Was that *actually* realistic —or was it more likely that I'd gone mad on the dirt floor of Baleros's cage after all his mind games?

It was obvious now. I'd imagined it all.

When Baleros had locked me in the dark iron box, I lived a million fantasy lives. This was just one of them.

How stupid to think I'd ever leave the iron box. And Ruadan was so perfect, the only explanation was that I'd dreamt him up. I was here again, trapped in an iron box. I'd be here forever.

Now that the fantasy world had been ripped away from me, the weight of my grief was so crushing I could hardly move. I was frozen, unable to move a finger or a toe.

There had been no Ruadan, no Institute, no special powers, no love, no mission to save the world. I could see nothing now except the inside of the iron box, and it burned my skin. I was here always and forever, Baleros's discarded toy.

I felt my soul ripping in two.

No. No. No.

It had to be real—I had to be real. Focus on my feet. My aching feet in the stupid high heels that came from the satyr and his stupid giant dick—

My consciousness ripped back out of the void, and I was standing in the church entryway again, certain that almost no time had passed at all. Just a hummingbird heartbeat. Merged with the shadow magic, I envisioned the shield shattering—and it did, like dark glass around me.

Gods below. That had nearly been a complete disaster.

Dangerous to give such a damaged person this much power. And that was the problem with me, wasn't it?

Still, I had to press on right now, before Ruadan lost the ability to cloak himself. I could hardly breathe as I touched the door handle. I turned the knob, and the door swung open into darkness.

I breathed in the scent of myrrh, my legs shaking wildly, knees weak. "Dad?"

Candles alit in their sconces and torches burst with golden light, illuminating the vaulted stone ceilings, the peaked arches and columns around the church. A trumpet song—a dirge—rang out, and my blood froze. Somehow I knew it heralded death. Then, the clopping of hooves echoed off the ceiling.

On his ashen horse, Adonis rode into the nave. Wings spread out, he loomed over this place of worship like a god. I stared into his pale eyes, flecked with gold, and his cold power hit me like a fist. His midnight wings swooped majestically behind him, the feathers shot through with silver, just as I remembered them.

I wanted so badly for him to call me "Bug," but this wasn't right.

I couldn't breathe. This wasn't the father I expected. This wasn't the man who'd held me in his lap and told me stories about birds who were bullied by larger birds and then made friends with kittens. This was not the man who'd wiped my runny nose or brought me water in the night. Not the man who'd stroked my hair and told me that monsters weren't real, even though he knew better than anyone what a lie that was.

No, this was Thanatos. This was my father as the Horseman. He rode his ashen horse into battle—his companion in the end of the world.

A powerful ally.... One that you know well.

It wasn't Nyxobas. My *father* was Baleros's ally.

I stared at the Horseman of Death. I knew just by looking at him, by the cold look in his eyes, that my father's seal had broken open. His curse had been released, the real Adonis lost forever.

I felt my heart breaking right there, and I wasn't sure it would ever heal.

Thick, red blood began streaming down the ancient flagstones beneath the horse's hooves.

Before me stood an ashen horse. Its rider was named Death, and Hell followed close behind him.

The wavering light gilded his coldly beautiful features, glinting in his eyes. He looked familiar and alien at the same time, and the contemptuous look on his face stopped me where I stood. A powerful sword hung at his waist, and he unsheathed it, hardly looking at me.

Sword in hand, he looked straight ahead, staring out the church doors. My heart felt like it was about to burst.

"Dad?"

My first thought was that this couldn't be him. My dad wouldn't just ignore me like this. But I could feel the death magic spiraling off him, and I could smell the myrrh. And worse, I could see the dark magic writhing around his throat —just over the necklace of red rose petals encased in amber that he always wore.

I wanted to throw up. The curse had overtaken him—the seal had opened, and the Horseman of Death had arrived. And he didn't even seem to know me.

Cora's words returned to me: the prophecy of the gods. *I looked, and behold, an ashen horse; and he who rode it had the name Death; and Hell followed him.*

As I stared at him, the monster inside me ached for release. My wings were ready to burst forth from my shoulder blades. He was here to kill, and I had the strongest urge to join him— to just give in to what I really was and to level the whole city.

I gritted my teeth, and I focused again on my feet on the

ground, trying to root myself in the reality of the situation. If the seal of Death had been opened, and if his curse had taken hold, was there actually any hope at all?

To my horror, I smelled something else in the ancient church, something besides the dark myrrh of my father. The sickly-sweet scent of roses. Baleros had been here. Baleros and the Horseman, working together.

"Dad?" I called out more desperately, hoping this time to get through to him. "Why are you here?"

He looked at me but didn't quite seem to see me, and he slowly guided his horse past me over the worn church flagstones. "Authority was given to me." His voice boomed off the ancient stone vaults. "To kill with sword and with famine and with pestilence and by the wild beasts of the earth."

A sob caught in my throat. This was not the reunion I'd been hoping for. What the hells was I supposed to do now? Our entire plan had hinged on finding my father, and finding him *sane*.

My pulse thundered through my veins. We were out of time.

My dad kicked his horse, galloping from the church, and the sound of clopping hooves echoed off the stone walls.

The breath left my lungs.

Ruadan. I didn't have any other plan right now except getting to Ruadan and keeping him safe. His disguise would wear off soon. Everything else would have to wait.

I charged into the churchyard after my father, then shadow-leapt backward on the route I'd mapped earlier.

There, in the center of Smithfield, was the god Nyxobas. Or at least, Ruadan disguised as Nyxobas. His body seemed to suck up light like a black hole, and the world darkened around him. Only his silver eyes gleamed from the vortex of magic. I leapt into the pool of shadows surrounding Ruadan, taking cover in the billowing darkness.

I tried not to look up at him, worried I'd lose my mind if I did. Instead, I closed my eyes and touched his cheek. "I found my dad, but the seal of death has been opened. He's cursed. I need you to leave here now—"

His hand was on the small of my back, pulling me into the vortex of darkness. I was dizzy again, overcome by the feeling that I'd imagined it all. I forced myself to focus on the high heels.

"I'm not leaving you with Baleros," he said. "We fight him together."

"He's not here. I'll try to deal with my father. But you need to—"

The smell of roses made my stomach twist, and I whirled around to see Baleros. His body trembled, but he was approaching the god all the same. He wore his usual clothing —the baggy wool getup of a Victorian showman.

"God of night." His dark eyes twinkled. "When my Angel of Death slaughters half the city, I will be sure to dedicate the souls to you, Nyxobas." He bowed with a strange flourish.

A surge of wild protectiveness shot through me like flame. I stepped out of Nyxobas's shadows. Baleros wanted to use my father to kill—and he'd be sure to count Ruadan among the dead.

There was no running from the Angel of Death if Baleros had him as an ally. One way or another, we had to end this now.

A ferocious fire burned in my heart, and my will to protect Ruadan hardened like volcanic rock. Dark magic flitted down my shoulder blades, sharp and smooth as a knife's edge. My wings burst out of me.

"Liora," Ruadan said from behind me. The shadows around him disappeared. He'd dropped the guise of Nyxobas.

Now there was nothing between Baleros and him but me.

I had no whiskey, now, to quell my most savage thoughts,

but Ruadan's serene magic brushed over my skin. I simply had no other options. I had to end this.

She had the name of Death, and Hell followed her.

My gaze flicked to the skies. My father was circling above, midnight wings resplendent as clouds gathered beyond him. I felt an overwhelming longing to follow him up there, to unleash destruction over the city.

My fingers twitched.

Baleros's eyes widened at the sight of me. A vision burst in my mind—the tip of my blade carving a horizontal slash across his chest, a vibrant splash of crimson, then a downward slash.

Then, the burst of flame that would revive him again.

"What did you do to my father?" I growled.

Baleros stared at me. "He's simply doing what he was born to do. The gods gave us all roles, didn't they? The monsters of death, the breakers of hearts."

"And what are you?" I asked.

"Me? I'm just here to put on a good show."

I drew my sword, desperate to slice him.

Kill by sword, famine, and plague, and by the wild beasts of the earth.

My death magic was ready to shoot from my ribs like hundreds of praying mantises bursting from an egg.

Woe to the people who dwell on this earth.

My father—cursed—swooped beneath the darkening skies overhead. Baleros was so close to getting what he wanted, but I'd never seen him looking so unsure before.

How do you threaten a man who revives himself?

"Where's my mother?" I asked.

Baleros shrugged. "Your mother, your entire village from Eden. I have them all. As long as you step away from the fomoire you're shielding, I'll return them all to you. Completely safe." He shoved his hands in his pockets, attempting to look composed, but I could see the sweat beading on his forehead. "And you'll have your father back, too. All I need is the World Key."

I tightened my grip on the hilt of my sword. "You're not getting Ruadan. I don't care how many times I have to kill you. I'm prepared to kill you over and over in increasingly creative ways, until the end of time. In fact, I've been looking for a hobby."

Ruadan stepped out from behind me, his sword glinting in the sunlight. "This sounds like leisure time we could both enjoy."

Baleros looked up at the skies again, eyes locking on my father, and nausea rose in my gut.

The beast climbs from a bottomless pit.

Baleros's dark eyes glistened. "Then you've made your choice. And of course you choose death. You're a monster, just like him." A mocking half-smile. Then, a subtle gesture— just a flick of his eyes up to the death god above. "I never should have let you out of—"

Ruadan lunged forward, driving his sword into Baleros's chest, ripping his body apart with brutally efficient violence.

I tore my gaze from Baleros's shattered body to look at my father. Had Baleros signaled to him?

The necklace—the red flowers around my father's neck— glowed with magic.

Trumpets blared, and darkness spilled out from his body.

CHAPTER 32

A star named Wormwood fell from the sky, poisoning the rivers. Hail, fire, and blood rain down on the earth, and the mountains crumble into the sea.

My toes curl with ecstasy and sulfur blasts from my mouth.

The explosion of death magic that hit me was a disturbingly pleasurable rush, perfect power trembling through my bones. Sulfur, blood, and ash clouded the air around me, and an overpowering scent of myrrh. Then, the smell of charring of flesh.

When the magic departed my blood, I was left with the taste of dust in my mouth, my limbs shaking with euphoria.

Even before the air cleared, I could feel it around me—the absence of life, the stillness of the hearts and blood. Leaves withering on their branches, grass wilting to a dry gray.

And most of all, grave silence.

Death reigned.

A small fire burned before me—the charred remains of Baleros's body. He'd rise again, a repulsive, corrupted phoenix from the ashes. No one else would.

I didn't want to look to my left. Ruadan lay there, his

heart no longer beating. I already felt his death—the absence of his magic in the air suffocated me. It was like someone had sucked the oxygen from the world. I felt like my soul had died with him.

My whole body had gone cold, fingers twitching.

I glanced up at the skies, where my father carved a vicious arc above London, feathers gleaming.

Then, slowly, I forced myself to turn my head.

Ruadan's perfect body lay curled like a child sleeping, his skin gray, chest no longer moving. His sword had fallen from his hand, glistening with gore. His pale hair hung in his face, and a cluster of wilted dandelions lay by one of his hands.

The sight of him broke me, and a strange quiet overtook my mind, silent and still as the dead lying around me. I wanted to lie down with them, and my body no longer wanted to move.

Nothing could kill my dad except my mum. I didn't really understand it except that she had some kind of magic from the Old Gods.

That meant I did, too. Right?

The angel—the creature once my father—circled overhead like a bird of prey. He wasn't my father now. He was the Horseman of Death.

I pulled a bow off one of the demons, and I ripped his quiver off him. I plucked an arrow out. The iron stung my fingers, but I pierced the tip of my finger with the arrowhead anyway. I'd poison it with my blood.

Then, I nocked the arrow, training the tip right on my father's heart.

Pure, heavy silence in my skull, dark as the clouds of ash above me. Only then did my hands stop shaking.

I loosed the arrow, and it shot through the air, finding its mark in his chest.

One shot, and the arrow tip—coated in my blood—

pierced his heart. The shot jolted him, and his wings seemed to carry him for a few moments. Then, he spiraled down to earth. A sharp chasm of grief split my chest, but my mind was too quiet to make sense of it. Something had broken in me; I'd moved into a place without language or meaning. Now, only instinct drove me.

I surveyed the ground around me, and a glint of metal on one of the demons' bodies caught my eye. I crossed to him, and I plucked a knife off his body. Then, from another fallen demon, I pulled an iron mace. Its heaviness felt perfect in my grip. That was what I needed for what would come next.

I scanned the ashy air around me.

Now, I needed the scent of roses.

Baleros was coming back, and he wouldn't stray far from the World Key. Some fierce, animal part of me wanted to protect Ruadan's body with all the fight I had left.

I sniffed the air, mentally sifting past the scents of myrrh, sulfur, blood, and decay. After a few moments, I found what I was searching for. The sickly-sweet rose petal scent among all the death.

The church again.

My powerful, black wings beat the air, carrying me toward the medieval church. The sooty wind tore at my hair as I flew, and it stung my eyes. But within moments, I was at the church doors.

I gripped the hilt of the knife as I crossed into the church. In the nave—where, just minutes before, I'd seen the Horseman of Death—I now found Baleros brushing ash off his clothes.

His head snapped up as I stalked toward him.

Vaguely, my brain recognized the look of terror on Baleros's face and that he'd gone pale as milk.

Only a heartbeat until I was before him.

First, I had to break his bones. That's where the mace

came in. Crouching, I swung it into his knees—the right one, the left. I vaguely registered his screams, that he was falling to the stone. I whirled, smashing into his ribs. I crushed his arms next.

Baleros was the one who'd taught me to use a mace—the brutal and precise swings, the blunt force.

When he lay crumpled and broken, bleeding onto the flagstones, I pulled out the knife. As if from a distance, I heard myself say, "You made me think I was a monster. But there's a difference between being a monster and a survivor. And that's what I am—a survivor."

Until now, I'd never really escaped that dirt cage—not completely. Because the rusted bars and crushing sense of worthlessness had lived on in my mind. All Baleros's lessons—the laws of power, my true nature—had lived in me. I'd carried the one central truth he'd imparted to me— that I was a monster. I'd never freed myself from that prison.

I'd always known that I'd never rid my mind of his voice until his heart stopped forever. And that was why he had to die.

The thing about Baleros was that he kept coming back. But the thing about the gods was they wanted nothing more than the souls that were due to them.

Whatever Baleros was screaming at me, I tuned it out. I'd broken most of his bones, and he wasn't going anywhere as I carved the symbol in his chest—the sigil of Nyxobas. Three pointed arrows, the moon, and a circle. Blood streamed down his chest.

When I'd finished making the mark of Nyxobas, I straddled him at the waist. I brought the knife down hard, sliding it just under his ribs to stop his heart.

A flicker of euphoria in my own chest. Then, I leapt off his carcass.

I stared as a white light bloomed from his body like smoke—his soul leaving his corpse.

I took a few more steps back as the gods appeared.

To my left, Emerazel's charcoal body appeared in the church in a blaze of flames, her skin cracked with fissures of lava. And to the right, the vortex of starry shadows, the icy eyes of the night god. Two ancient enemies, one miserable little soul.

The gods hardly noticed me, this angel of death in their midst. I took another step back and stared as the two gods grasped for Baleros's soul, greedy as children fighting over a piece of cake.

They ripped his worthless soul in two, tearing it down the middle like an old rag. My old gladiator master, forever shredded, never again to be whole.

I kept the knife from Baleros's chest, my own little macabre trophy, and I rolled it between my fingers. The weight of Baleros's lessons evaporated off my body like a lifted curse.

The smell of rot filled the air, and I frowned. More death —here in the church?

I traced my fingertips over the stone walls as I followed the scent of death out of the church, the smell drawing me like a candle flame draws a moth.

I stalked out of the church, an angel of death covered in the blood of her old master. I crossed under the vaulted arches to the cloisters. I pushed through the door, and the scent of death hit me like a fist.

That's where I found them—the inhabitants of Eden. They lay in piles on the cloister floor, iron chains around their bodies.

It took me a few moments to find my mother's vibrant red hair, covering her purpled face. Her body was hunched over on the stones. All this was Baleros's work. His master-piece—his greatest show.

Too bad there was no one left to watch it.

Still, that eerie silence in my skull, quiet as a pile of bones....

I still held tight to that knife, slick with Baleros's blood.

With my wings cascading behind me, I crossed out of the church. Out here, the ashen landscape of death mirrored my state of mind. I wanted to join the dead.

That's when the grief slammed into me, a knife-sharp split in my chest, the pain so intense I could hardly think. It was like my heart had been hewn from my chest. My ribs had turned to iron spikes. My body was punishing me for continuing to breathe while Ruadan didn't. Ruadan's secrets would die along with him. His childhood in Emain, the memories of his brothers—all dead with him.

With that acrid burst of death magic from my father, I had no doubt that the knights of the Tower were lying dead now, too. Bodies rotting in their cowls.

London was a mass grave.

My own death magic was ready to burst out of me and rain all over the earth, just as my father's had done—

It took a few moments for the words to come back into my mind so I could understand things again. Red hair, my mother's slumped body. This was the second time I'd seen my mother dead—both times from the Plague. That particular death magic that my father and I possessed.

Dead twice.

Now, my thoughts were roaring in my skull, the noise deafening. That tiny, red ember lit in my heart again.

But Baleros's voice wasn't there in the din. Just mine, now.

Red hair, spread out over the dirt.

My father had brought my mother back, hadn't he? He'd

brought them all back from the shadow hell after they died of plague. I had my father's powers. We could reverse this magic. Both of us could reverse it.

Fix it, then.

My wings lifted me into the air. The hollowness of my chest had knife-sharp edges. I needed to fill it with something. I swooped over Ruadan's body, taking in the wilted flowers in his fist. The sight of him ripped me apart once more.

I needed to fix it, just as Nyxobas had said.

My chest was an empty vessel as I hovered above him.

The name Liora—it meant *my light.* They'd called me that because I had my mother's light, and now a fiery light began to burn brighter, deep inside me.

I let a vision dance in my mind of Ruadan threading together dandelion wreaths, of him hunting in the forest with a spear he'd made for himself. I could almost feel our fingers entwining once more.

His essence—that savage serenity—poured into the hollowness in my chest. It curled around my ribs, easing some of that sharpness, warming me. As Ruadan's essence filled me, so too did the death magic all around me. I was pulling it into me, feeding from it. My back arched, and I drew the magic out of the dead around me.

I let the toxins fill me with spirals of dark power. Then, my wings lifted me higher in the cloudy, sulfurous skies.

My father's myrrh-scented magic whirled into me, filling the void between my ribs. Power infused my limbs and wings, spreading out from my heart, down my shoulder blades, snapping through my bones. It shot down my arms, my legs, until it reached the ends of my toes and my fingertips. My chest swelled as the deaths of everything around me flowed into me.

The deaths of all those around me—the demons, the fae, the knights in the Tower—they all poured into me.

I could feel life slowly returning around me—the withered leaves turning green again, faint pulses starting to beat in veins. Tiny puffs of breath filled still lungs, and skin began to warm.

Ruadan.

I soared down once more. My eyes were on Ruadan's body as the color returned to him and one of his fingers twitched.

A low, almost inaudible beat—the pulse of blood. A heart's pumping. Then, Ruadan's electrical magic crackled in the air.

All around me, life stirred. The lungs of demons filled with air. Somewhere, I was certain my mother was stirring among the bodies in the cloister, pushing her red hair out of her eyes once more.

But right now, I was angling my flight towards Ruadan. And I wouldn't feel whole again until our limbs were intertwined, chests pressed together, hearts beating in unison. I threaded my fingers into his hair, and I pressed my lips to his. This was where I was meant to be.

My wings slid back into my body, and I pulled away from the kiss to look at Ruadan.

He stared at me, stunned, irises black as pitch. "You brought me back."

"Baleros is dead. For good," I murmured into his neck. "And we're never again going to part."

CHAPTER 33

*J*knelt by my mum, and we stared at each other. She looked exactly the same—same pistachio-green eyes, porcelain skin. Same cherry-red hair. I'd changed drastically, but she'd been preserved like a perfect blossom in amber. She was even wearing one of her glamorous dresses: gold beads and gossamer threads. Tiny blue gemstones gleamed from her forehead.

She cocked her head, frowning as if unwilling to believe I was real. Then, light beamed from her features, and her eyes glistened. She touched my cheek. "Liora?"

I didn't know what to say. How did we recap everything that had happened? *So, I killed you, then ran away to become enslaved, and then a Knight of the Shadow Fae arrived and we had to find a satyr's penis and....* Instead, I just said, "Yeah."

She grabbed onto me so tight I thought my ribs would crack, and I thought, for a moment, her claws had come out. Her loud sobs echoed off the walls, and her tears wet my shoulder. Around me, I heard the sound of chains breaking as Ruadan freed the other fae.

I wrapped my arms around her. She was smaller than me

now. How had that happened? The last time I saw her, I could still fit in her lap and rest my head on her shoulder when I was upset. Now, I felt like I could break her. Her hug was ferocious. Mine was gentle.

Through her sniffles, she let out a long breath. "When did you get so big?"

I pressed my face into her neck. "Some time in the past dozen years, I guess."

Her fingertips brushed over my upper arm. "How did you get this scar?"

Oh, Mum. That was one of dozens. "Long story."

She pulled away, narrowing her eyes at me. "Did anyone try to hurt you after you left Eden?" The fierceness in her voice actually made me jolt.

I just shrugged. "I'm fine."

She nodded. "Right. I want you to tell me everything that happened since I last saw you. Everything. Every day and every hour."

"I will. I promise. In a bit. Are you okay, though? You were just ... dead."

"You killed me again, didn't you?"

I wiped a tear off my cheek. "Oh, I see. Just coming right out with the murder accusations thirty seconds into our reunion?"

"It's the second time you've hit me with your death magic. Your father's going to have to teach you to control it."

That sharp fissure of grief started to open in my chest again as I realized she didn't know about Adonis, and I was going to have to tell her.

"It wasn't me," I said. "This time, I mean. It was Dad. Or, rather, the Horseman of Death. I brought you all back, just like he did when I killed you."

She went still, her body rigid. "What?"

219

"His seal has been opened. He turned into the Horseman of Death. I had to kill him. His body is in Smithfield, outside."

She arched an eyebrow at me, the look a mum gave when she thought you were full of shit but didn't want to say so. A long sigh. "Oh, Liora." The disappointment in her voice made me feel terrible. She gripped my shoulders so hard I was certain she'd leave bruises. "None of what you're saying makes sense."

"I know what I'm talking about," I said defensively, feeling suddenly like a child who'd just reported a monster under my bed. "I just did a whole death angel thing and brought everyone back from the dead."

Gripping my hand hard, she pulled me toward the churchyard. I shot a helpless look at Ruadan, following her lead.

"First of all," my mum said, "I pulled the curse off him long ago. He can't be cursed."

We'd only just become reunited, and I already wanted to argue with my mum. "He killed everyone, Mum. I saw him in the church, and he said some creepy stuff about killing with swords and beasts. He barely looked at me, then he flew out into the skies. The air smelled of sulfur and blood, and then he unleashed his death magic. That's how you died."

"Second of all," she went on, ignoring my airtight arguments, "you can't kill him. Only I can."

Granted, I was less certain of this one. The blood thing had been a guess. "I thought maybe my blood would kill him, because you can kill him, and I came from you."

She shook her head, practically dragging me into Smithfield. "It's not my blood that could kill him. It's the magic in these." She pointed at the tiny gemstones in her forehead. "I'm sure you did some damage, Liora, but you didn't kill him. He'll be fine."

I frowned. "Okay, fine. But he had *definitely* turned evil."

"Evil, yes. Cursed, no." She beamed at me. "Liora, what have you been doing all this time? I can't believe how big you are."

My throat was tight. "We can go over that later. How did you end up in the cloisters?"

"Nyxobas found his way through the glamour. He knocked out our entire village with his sleep magic a few weeks ago. I woke up chained and soaking wet in the cloisters, and your father was gone. That's all I know. I've hardly eaten anything in weeks."

We drew closer to my father, who lay flat on his back in the square. The arrow I'd shot him with protruded from his chest. Blood streamed from it. He'd gone completely still.

My mum looked back at me with pride. "Did you shoot him down from the air? Well done, Liora. You weren't that good with a bow and arrow last time I saw you. You'd hardly used one."

I blinked at her. What was even real right now? "Um, I feel you might not be taking this situation as seriously as you should be."

She fixed her green eyes on mine. "Your father can't die unless I kill him. And even if that happened, you could bring him back, just like he brought you back weeks ago. You have that power over each other." She took another step closer, inspecting me carefully. "That's why I always knew you were okay. At least until a few weeks ago, when someone killed you. Your father had to bring you back. What happened then, exactly?"

I swallowed hard. "His name was Baleros, and he was a monster." I gestured around me. "He's responsible for all this. For Nyxobas taking you out of Eden. For whatever happened to Dad. A whole bunch of shit. But he's dead now."

"You killed him?"

I nodded. "For good this time."

That pride shone from her face again, along with the gleaming of the gemstones in her forehead. Despite everything I'd been through, I felt as proud as she looked.

My mum knelt next to my father's body. His wings spread out beneath him—the darkest blue, feathers shot through with strands of silver.

"But like I said," my mum added, "you didn't kill him."

Something I hadn't noticed before now caught my eye— the faintest hint of shadow magic glowed around the necklace he wore, the one with a flower encased in amber. I knelt by his side, staring at the necklace. It was so faint I could hardly see it, but it was there—a vague midnight glimmer of shadow magic. Just like Baleros had used on Barry. Baleros had used his magic to control the both of them.

"I think I found the problem." I reached around his throat and unclasped the necklace. I lifted it into the air, the crimson flower glinting in the sunlight.

Soft footsteps sounded behind me, and I smelled Ruadan's piney approach, felt his magic curling around me. He leaned down and plucked the necklace from my hand, then rolled it over between his fingertips. "Nyxobas charmed this."

My mum stared at Ruadan, eyes hard as flint. "Who's this ancient fae, exactly?"

I cleared my throat. "That's a long story, really…. There are a lot of … really just a lot of misunderstandings over the years—"

My mum looked like she was about to go feral. "He's too old for you."

My mouth opened and closed, and I considered pointing out that the Horseman of Death lying before us was several thousand years older than she was.

Ruadan looked her directly in the eye. "I'm Ruadan,

Prince of Emain, Grand Master of the Shadow Fae Institute. I saw you years ago when I—"

"I have an idea," I said, interrupting this reminiscence before he got to the *tried to kill your husband* part. Ruadan had many beautiful qualities, but tact wasn't his strong suit. "How about we get the arrow out of my dad's chest, and then we can chat about all the fun memories later."

Ruadan cocked his head, then nodded. "Yes."

I looked down at my dad's perfect face, the dark sweep of lashes and straight black eyebrows. Already, I could tell my mother was right. The arrow had stopped his heart, but there was still life in him. His skin still had a healthy glow.

I gripped the iron shaft, then yanked it from his chest. With his eyes still closed, he took a deep breath. Then, his eyes opened, and I leaned over him to look into them—the sapphire and gold of my memory.

A little crease formed between his dark eyebrows.

"Dad. I'm sorry I...." I swallowed hard. "Shot you out of the sky." I bit my lip. "Although you were killing everyone, so...."

He beamed at me, drawing me close into his arms. "Bug."

I breathed in the scent of myrrh. He wasn't a monster— and neither was I.

CHAPTER 34

On top of one of the Institute's towers, I sat on a blanket between my mum and my dad. We were drinking wine out of silver goblets, and we stared up at the spray of stars across the sky. Their bodies warmed mine, and I plucked another strawberry from the bowl before us.

"And that's how I became the amazing sword fighter I am today." The pride in my voice was evident.

After several hours, I'd finally finished telling them about what I'd been doing since I'd last seen them.

"A *gladiator?*" The rage in my father's voice ruined the serenity of the moment. "A *slave?*"

"It wasn't that bad," I lied. "I made a good friend. Ciara. And then I got out." I left out the iron box and the sweets. I was done with that part of my life, now, and there was no need to keep reliving it.

A few clouds began gathering on the horizon, covering the moon.

"I want to raise Baleros from the dead and kill him again," said my dad.

"Can you do that?" I asked.

"No," he admitted.

"Tell me again why we're not supposed to kill Ruadan," said my mum. "He came into Eden to kill us. He took you away from us."

I heaved a sigh. "I already told you. He didn't take me away. I ran through the portal because I thought Dad had killed everyone, since you'd never before told me he was an angel. And Ruadan didn't know what he was getting into, either, when he came to Eden. He thought he was coming for an angel, and that was it. Not the Horseman. And moreover, I love him, and he loves me."

Silence fell, broken only by the sound of the wind rushing over the parapet.

"I feel safe with him," I added.

We could have argued, I supposed, about whose fault it was that the worlds closed at all—was it the Institute's? Was it my father's? Instead, they let my last words hang in the air for another minute.

My mum watched me pull another strawberry from the bowl. "Since when did you start eating strawberries?"

I took a bite. "What?"

"You don't eat strawberries," my father added. "You hardly eat any fruit."

"Or meat," my mum added.

"Just bread and butter," said my dad. "If you weren't immortal, I'd worry about your health."

"And milk," my mum added. "You always need milk at night at three in the morning."

It was quickly becoming clear that their image of me would be stuck in the distant past, at least for a while. I might look completely different, but in their minds, I was still a child. I was still young enough to wake them up at night with nightmares.

And for just a few minutes, I liked it that way.

There was still time for them to get used to me—the adult me, the one who could take care of herself. We were immortals, and we'd get around to it. But for this night, I was just their daughter again.

They'd have to return to their own world at some point, but with Ruadan at my side, I'd be able to see them whenever I wanted. I'd have my family back.

* * *

I LAY ALONE in the bed I shared with Ruadan, wrapped in our silky sheets. Three months had passed since I'd found my parents again, since I'd pulled the death magic off Ruadan and the Knights.

Three months of pure bliss.

Through his magic, Ruadan had lured me into sleeping in an actual bed, like a civilized person.

Outside, the setting sun cast ginger rays over periwinkle clouds. Night would fall over the Institute's ancient riverside towers soon.

I closed my eyes, thinking of the moment I'd brought him back from the dead.

The truth was, caring for other people could make you vulnerable, but it could make you strong, too—like the mums who suddenly develop the strength of a superhero to lift a car off their toddlers. My love for Ruadan had turned me into someone who could heal, not just kill.

A knock sounded on the door, and I wrapped a bed sheet around myself. Then, I crossed to the door.

I pulled it open to find Ruadan there. He was dressed in his finest black clothes, and they fitted beautifully over his powerful body. Light from the setting sun washed him in hues of gold.

He held out a flowered wreath to me.

"What's this?"

"Moonflowers for the night realm, columbines for faith-fulness, myrtle for love, and yew leaves for death. I couldn't ignore the monstrous side that I love."

I took it from him, smiling. Something ivory flashed in the wreath. My nose wrinkled. "Did you put bones in this?"

"Bits of tusk from an Emain boar."

"Right. And what is that about?"

He frowned. "They're just large feral pigs, basically."

I blinked at him, and it took me a moment to remember that Ruadan had an extremely dry and extremely strange sense of humor sometimes.

Then, a smile danced over his lips. "They represent your ferocity and mine."

So he thought of me a *bit* like a feral pig. Ruadan was not the best with tact, but I loved him anyway. "Well, it's strange and perfect."

His gaze swept over me. "You're not dressed."

"It's a good thing I'm not. It's bad luck to see a bride in her dress before the wedding. How much time do we have?"

"The sun will set in about twenty minutes."

"Best leave me to get dressed, then. I'll meet you outside, when I'm making you my husband."

Of course, only a moonlight wedding would do for the Shadow Fae.

I glanced at the dress hanging on the wall. My mum had made it, of course. Dresses were more her thing than mine. It was the thinnest of materials, ephemeral and gorgeous, with tiny flecks of glittering, pale blue gems, just like the ones in her forehead.

I pulled it on and inched it down over my hips. The silky material fitted me perfectly—tight around the hips, but with enough room that I could move my legs—and the lace sleeves showed off my strong arms. My mum had done well. Even the high-heeled shoes matched the dress perfectly, though I could hardly walk in them.

I lifted the crown of flowers to my head, then turned to look at myself in the mirror. I smiled. No one did glamour like my mum, and I looked perfect. I couldn't wait to see the look on Ruadan's face, although I knew he liked me well enough in tattered, bloodied clothes anyway.

A last ray of amber light caught my eyes before the sun slipped behind the horizon completely.

"I … a darkness. Dick." A deep voice turned my head. Demented Mike stood in the door holding a flower out to me —a red anemone, just like the ones that grew on the river-bank in Eden. "For you." He smiled. "Happy."

I crossed to him and plucked it from his hand, smiling. "Thanks, Mike. We need to get you some more of that magic tea."

He shoved his hands in his pockets and turned, saun-tering down the hallway, whistling. It was weirdly good to see him again, even if we still needed to work on his language skills.

I turned back to the mirror and threaded the red flower into my crown. It was only another moment before more footsteps sounded down the hall and Melusine poked her head in the door.

Then, just beside her, Ciara's freckled face, grinning.

"You guys can come in," I said. "For a minute." I peered out the window at the chairs arranged on the Tower Green in two rows of semicircles. Guests were already starting to arrive and fill them, their jewels gleaming in the twilight.

Ciara lay on my bed. She wore a pink dress with puffy sleeves and sequins, and I had no idea where she had found it, but it looked several decades old and distinctly human. She propped herself up on her elbows, staring at me dreamily. "You look beauuuuutiful. I could just light you on fire. Grrrrrrr, why does beauty make me feel aggressive?"

I wrinkled my nose. "Please don't light me on fire." Ruadan was letting her live here at the Institute with us—and so far, a little fire magic had come in handy among the Shadow Fae.

Melusine held a long bit of gossamer fabric in her hands. "I see a wedding dress, I think the wedding is about to start. I put two and two together. But you need your veil."

"I'm glad I have you here, then," I said.

I faced the window while Melusine pinned the veil to my floral crown. "What's this made out of?" I asked.

"Spider silk, woven by the dungeon spiders."

"I did not know we had dungeon spiders." I still had so much to learn about this ancient fortress....

I stared through the aged glass panes at Ruadan, who drank from a silver cup. For once, he was the one who seemed to be fortifying himself with alcohol instead of me.

My parents were out there—standing as far as they could from Ruadan's mother, Queen Macha. Gods, she still scared the shite out of me. My mother-in-law for the rest of eternity, a woman who fed off the violent subjugation of her enemies.

Well, maybe we could just avoid her.

It was at this point I realized that I had no idea how this wedding ceremony was going to work. I assumed I'd just walk down an aisle with flowers or something, but the chairs in semicircles were throwing me off. "What exactly is going to happen at this wedding, Melusine?" If anyone would know the details, it would be Melusine.

"That's right. You weren't raised among the fae nobility,"

C.N. CRAWFORD

Melusine pointed out. "So you have no idea. It starts with the music. Then there's the twining. Then the spirits of the fallen return to pay their respects. Then there's the dancing, eating, and more dancing for seven days, during which time everyone calls you 'queen.' That does not continue after the seven days, so don't get used to it."

I cleared my throat. "Sorry, what's the *twining?*"

"Oh, well, you'll find out soon." She nodded at the window. "The moon is out. Time to start."

I took a deep breath. All of a sudden, I was more nervous than I'd been before my gladiator matches. Gods, give me a sword and a mace and someone to kill and I knew exactly what I needed to do. A wedding ceremony surrounded by fae nobility—and a literal queen—had me trembling as I walked.

At the base of the Tower, I pulled open the door to the green.

Ciara and Melusine pushed past me, then ran frantically through the grass to get to their seats. I heaved a deep breath, trying to find Ruadan through the dim light. I couldn't see him there, and I still had no real sense of what I was supposed to do.

I took one step, then another, feeling wobbly in my high heels. Frowning, I decided I needed to ditch the heels. They weren't me. I kicked them off, hiked the dress up a bit so I could walk more freely, and just started strutting toward the center of the circle, hoping everything would work out—the confident gait of a warrior. I was meeting Ruadan there, and that was all that mattered.

As I walked, the strange fae music swelled—strings and drums that vibrated over my skin.

Everyone was watching me—my dad, my mum, Aengus, and Aenor and Cora, who were gripping each other's arms and grinning like giddy children. Queen Macha in her gleaming crown was smoking a *cigar*, blowing smoke rings and glaring at me. I had not seen that one coming.

I saw Ruadan just as the moonlight hit his perfect features, and he beamed at me, radiant and perfect as the night sky. The love in his eyes was pure magic.

Apparently, we had seven days of music, eating, and dancing ahead of us, but I would make it my mission to drag Ruadan back to our room as much as I could, and to wrap myself around him. My mind whirled with visions of our future—fighting side by side, sleeping in the same bed. Maybe children. Had we talked about children? We hadn't. Did he want children? Did I want children? I thought I did, but how would I fight demons with a giant pregnant stomach? So many questions.

But as soon as I reached him, that soothing magic whispered over my skin, and the chaos in my mind began to calm and still. Ruadan wrapped his arms around me and whispered into my ear that he loved me.

As he did, shadow magic twined around us, binding us together. Then, ropes of vines sprouted from the earth and encircled our bodies, rooting us to the earth and to each other. The plants wound firmly around us. So *this* was the twining, I supposed.

I had no idea what I was meant to do, so I pushed up onto my tiptoes and kissed Ruadan on the mouth. We were two broken monsters, now healed.

If I was a raging ocean wave, he was the dark quiet underneath. And we were perfect for each other.

* * *

THANK you for reading Court of Dreams.

The next books in the series continue on with prequel

books that tell the story of Adonis and Ruby, and of the apocalypse that started it all.

Thanks so much for reading our books.

We have a number of series set in the *Demons of Fire and Night World,* including *Vampire's Mage* and *Shadows and Flame.* If you want to be introduced to some of the other characters in our series, you can download our free stories here.

https://dl.bookfunnel.com/ge0bq4cyhg

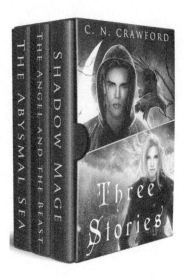

Also, check out our webpage for the full listing of books www.cncrawford.com

Also, please join our super fun Facebook group!

ACKNOWLEDGMENTS

Thanks to Michael Omer for his fantastic feedback and emotional support as always.

Robin and Isabella are my amazing editors. Thanks to my advanced reader team for their help, and to C.N. Crawford's Coven on Facebook!

ALSO BY C.N. CRAWFORD

For a full list of our books, check out our website.
https://www.cncrawford.com/books/

And a possible reading order.
Characters from Institute of the Shadow Fae appear in other series.
https://www.cncrawford.com/faq/